BOY

BOY

TAKESHI
KITANO

Translated by David James Karashima

VERTICAL.

Published by Vertical, Inc., New York.

Originally published in Japanese as *Shonen*
by Shinchosha, Tokyo, 1987.

ISBN 1-932234-35-7 / 978-1-932234-35-0

Manufactured in the United States of America

First Edition

Vertical, Inc.
1185 Avenue of the Americas 32nd Floor
New York, NY 10036
www.vertical-inc.com

CONTENTS

BOY

The Champion in a Padded Kimono

It had been two years since I'd last seen my brother.

For most of the year, he was out of Japan on business, but since we'd reached our thirties and started families of our own, we'd found ourselves wanting to catch up with each other once in a while. I don't remember who had suggested it first, but we decided to go for drinks at my friend's restaurant in Yotsuya.

My brother was in his forties now, and with his hair looking a lot thinner, it seemed he was taking after our old man. His face had filled out somewhat, but it didn't have the look of a man in the prime of his career. Instead it had the look of someone who was a good father. We'd been sharing stories about workplace and family, laughing and nodding at each other's remarks, when my brother leaned forward and asked me, "Do you play, Mamoru?" imitating a golf swing in a way that seemed to suggest that he himself played regularly.

"So you golf now, too?"

"Yeah, I do. I started on the recommendation of a colleague."

Then he took another swing with his imaginary club, while looking a little embarrassed. This was news to me. Although I wasn't surprised by his swing, there seemed to be something not quite right about it. In fact, I was willing to guess that he was terrible at the game.

Ever since he was young, my brother had always hated any kind of sport, and he'd always come last in his class in things like running races. And although he got A's in all his other classes, he always got a "D" in Physical Education. My mother always said that he actually deserved an "F", but that the teacher gave him a "D" out of pity.

"So what do you shoot?" I asked.

"Oh, I've only just started. How about you? I bet you shoot about 45 for nine holes."

"About that, maybe a bit better. And you?"

"Oh, it's not even worth mentioning."

"Why not? Come on, tell me. Have you completed nine holes in under 50 yet?"

"50 for nine holes isn't anything to be ashamed of you know."

"So you're that good already?"

"Actually, no. My average is more like 75." And with that he started to laugh. Of course, it wasn't like he'd made any great joke, but his laughter was contagious and in no time I was laughing too.

"Let's go golfing sometime, Mamoru." He said, catching his breath. "You could teach me. I really don't know why I can't…"

As I merrily listened to my brother inviting

me to play golf, my thoughts drifted back to an autumn day almost thirty years ago.

Soft sunlight was pouring in through the classroom windows and dancing on the floors. Outside, red dragonflies were hopping between the top of the exercise bars, the drinking fountains, and the instrument shed.

It looked like someone had sprinkled musical notes all over the field. I rested my head on my hand and just took it all in.

"Mamoru!" there came a shout. "Pay attention!"

Mr. Kondo's deep voice reverberated around the classroom and my elbow slipped off the desk in surprise, letting my chin smack down on the desk, and causing all the other children to burst out laughing.

"You idiot! What are you doing, Mamoru?

If I catch anyone else sitting around with a blank, idiotic look on their face at tomorrow's march-in, then that someone is going to get a fist in the head."

"Yes, Mr. Kondo," responded the whole class in soft unison as they imagined Mr. Kondo delivering one of his infamous "Thunderbolt Noogies" that seemed to drill right into your head.

"What's that? I can't hear you!"

"Yes, Mr. Kondo" came the reply from everyone, although louder this time.

"Well that's all for today. Make sure you get plenty of rest for tomorrow. Don't stop off anywhere on the way home, or buy something that's going to give you a stomach ache—especially you, Mamoru, that'd be just the kind of thing you would do."

I tutted to myself quietly but kept my eyes

on the textbook on his desk as angry thoughts whirled round in my head. *How dare he pick on me so much! He's just being big-headed because it's Sports Day tomorrow. So typical of him to take it all too seriously!*

"You look like you want to say something, Mamoru."

"No sir."

"Good. All right then, those of you running in the relay should get to bed especially early. I want you to be sure to beat Homeroom Three tomorrow. All right?"

No matter whether it was Sports Day or swim meets, Mr. Kondo always hated losing to the homeroom next door. At the summer swim meet, we'd lost to Homeroom Three in the 100 meter relay, so he'd made us sit on our knees for hours in the classroom, then lie down on our desks to practice the crawl. Who knew what kind of "self-reflection" we'd have to put up with if we dared to lose again.

Of course, he had a reason for acting this way and everyone knew about it; he'd been dumped by Homeroom Three's teacher, Miss Hanada. He'd gotten together with her as soon as she'd arrived at our school fresh from graduation at a women's university. But after just a few months it had been all over. Some of the girls in our class felt sorry for Mr. Kondo, but the majority of us felt this prickly man with scrubbing-brush hair had never really been in the league of someone like Miss Hanada with her stylish bobbed hair.

Mr. Kondo strode out of the classroom clutching a textbook in one hand. And behind him, everyone else followed. It was impossible for us all not to get excited about Sports Day—

after all, it only came around once a year. I was excited, too. In fact, maybe more so than anyone.

"Mamoru, pay attention!" called Kenji in his best Mr. Kondo voice as he came running up the hallway.

"Shut up."

"Relay runners should go straight home to bed," added Yutaka, who'd also just caught up.

"You're running the relay, too," I said. "Why don't you get on straight home to bed!"

Yutaka and myself were two of the four people selected to be on the homeroom relay team. Unfortunately, my best friends Kenji and Toru hadn't made the selection, but everyone was feeling excited anyway and we couldn't even wipe the smiles off our faces when we got into an argument.

Out on the school field, about twenty teachers and fifth and sixth graders responsible for sports day were busy with final preparations. White tents had been put up on both sides of the morning assembly podium, gates had been set up and marked "Entrance" and "Exit", and white lines for the Sports Day events were being drawn out in chalk, including six lanes for the sprints that had been neatly drawn diagonally across the field. I loved that smell of chalk. It was the smell of the day where I could display my abilities and make up for my poorer performance in my studies. Academically, I had always been nearer the bottom of the class. But when it came to speed and athletic ability, I was at least second or third in my class.

As I watched the white lines being drawn on the ground, I could picture myself crossing the finish line in first place. I considered my strategy for the next day. I'd start off slow on purpose. Then, with about 20 meters left, I'd race out in front. That would look so much cooler than leading right from the start.

Me and my friends stepped behind the starting line, which was clearly marked with numbers, and we got down to practice our starts. Other students were chasing each other around the 200-meter track.

THUMP!

Suddenly, I felt an eye-popping blow on top of my head. Then a loud voice: "Mamoru, don't mess up the chalk lines!"

It was Mr. Kondo, of course, standing behind me with a fierce expression on his face.

"Shoot!" I said to myself and pulled my head down in preparation for the next punch. But the second "thunderbolt" never came. Slowly, I looked up to where Mr. Kondo was standing and I noticed him staring at Miss Hanada who was over near the exit gate.

Seeing a window of opportunity, Kenji shouted "Run!" and we all dashed off. Then, once we were outside the school gates, Kenji and the others started teasing me again.

"Don't mess up the chalk lines, thump!"

They imitated Mr. Kondo's voice and the way he brought his fist down over and over again. Then after having had a good laugh about it, Kenji tried to cheer me up by saying, "I bet Airhead's going to win by a mile again this year."

Airhead was in the sixth grade and he was always the champion on Sports Day. There wasn't a single person in school that didn't know who he was. And there were rumors that he was actually supposed to be in the second year of junior high, but I don't know if that was really true. He was hopeless when it came to studying and there were all kinds of rumors about him. Some people had said he couldn't even write his own name in kanji characters, that he had once gotten lost on the way back home from school, or that he'd been seen trying to read a book upside down. But when it came to sports, he was always in a league of his own. So despite his unflattering nickname, he was actually quite well respected. Fortunately, my brother Shinichi happened to be in the same homeroom as Airhead, so I always had the scoop on what was happening with him.

"Airhead was amazing in last year's final relay," Yutaka said in a tone that could have been taken as both awe and bewilderment. "I mean, he passed five people, and still had time to wave to the crowd."

"That guy's amazing," said Toru, his voice rising. "I bet he could even beat guys in junior high."

"Well actually, my brother told me that Airhead is off sick with a cold," I interrupted. "It seems he has a high fever. He might not be able to take part in field day at all."

"Huh?"

"You're kidding, right? That guy would never catch a cold."

"No, I'm not. He might even have to go to the hospital."

"That would spoil all the fun."

The three of them sounded deeply disappointed. And I felt the same way.

"Sports Day won't be any fun if Airhead isn't going to be there. But I bet he'll come even if he does have a fever."

"I'll bet. I mean, he's Airhead! He'll get over his cold and cruise to victory again," Yutaka said, gazing out into the distance.

"You know, Airhead really is amazing. But your brother, on the other hand, he's really slow isn't he, Mamoru? Airhead could probably beat him hopping on one leg."

With that, Toru picked up one ankle and started bobbing around.

"Don't be such a jerk!" I shouted at him, but my voice was drowned out among everyone's giggles.

The autumn sun was already beginning to set, stretching long shadows across the field from the two-story wooden school building, the exercise bars, the tents and the gingko trees. And as the teachers and students made their final preparations for the next day, they carried their long silhouettes around their legs.

"Hey, let's go to Goggle-eyed Gran's place and buy baseball photos," shouted Kenji. "Nagashima and Kawakami weren't included in the pack I bought the other day. Why don't we steal a few packs?" Kenji suggested like always.

"We can't. We just got caught the other day

and the old bag told us not to come back," said Yutaka, understandably unenthusiastic.

"Come on, she'll have forgotten by now. There was this one time when I got caught stealing in the morning, but when I went back that same afternoon, she welcomed me in, no problem."

The decision was made. We ran to the store, our school bags bouncing against our backs.

"Hello boys," said Goggle-eyed Gran in her usual voice.

Kenji turned and glanced at us, his eyes saying, "See, she's forgotten." Then we all went into the shop together.

Inside, there were all kinds of snacks, lucky draws, *menko* cards and spinning tops, although the floor space of the whole shop couldn't have been more than three tatami mats. Goggle-eyed Gran sat at the back of the store wearing a dark red, sleeveless vest covered in fuzzballs. She would grunt and get up, then come over to the kids when they wanted to have a go at one of the games like the one where you drew strings for different-sized strawberry candies. Occasionally, she'd cheat by giving us a different strawberry candy from the one we had drawn. Or if we'd won a winning ticket in the raffle, she'd say, "Oh, this one doesn't count," and throw it away. But nevertheless, this was the shop we all liked to come to.

Seeing me and the others looking at the photos of the sluggers Nagashima and Kawa-kami, Goggle-eyed Gran stood up.

"Tomorrow's your Sports Day, isn't it?" she said.

We all turned around to see her stretching out her wrinkly hands to show us some red object.

"You should buy this," she said.

"What is it?"

"It's chocolate. But it's no ordinary chocolate. It's special chocolate. If you eat it, it will definitely help you win at Sports Day tomorrow."

"No way."

I looked at Kenji, Yutaka and Toru as if to say, "Come on, we're not going to fall for this, right?"

But the three of them were staring at her palm as if they'd been put under a spell.

Unlike the regular Meiji-brand chocolate bar that was wrapped in brown paper and silver foil, this particular one was wrapped in red paper and had kanji characters on it that none of us knew how to read. And because Goggle-eyed Gran was stroking it so preciously, it somehow seemed to us like it was even more special.

Perhaps sensing my suspicion, she said, "If you don't believe me, don't buy it. Though I should tell you one of the sixth graders just came and bought one. What a shame, though. What a shame."

Then she shot a sideways glance at us before turning her back.

Toru, who wasn't a very good runner, was the first to call out. "No, wait. I'll buy it!" Then straight after him, Kenji, Yutaka and I said we wanted one, too.

On seeing the speed with which Goggle-eyed Gran turned around, it was difficult to believe she was really such an old woman.

"Okay, okay. It's 20 yen for one." And she went from one of us to the next taking the coins and handing over the chocolate.

"Now you're all set. You're all sure to come in first place tomorrow!"

Distracted by what had just happened, we left the shop without buying the card of Naga-shima. I think we all felt like we might have just been fooled.

Eager to try it out, I said, "Well, I guess we should eat it then!"

"Don't you think it will have more of an effect if we eat it right before we run?" said Toru, stroking his bar of chocolate, just like Goggle-eyed Gran.

"You're probably right."

Then, just as I'd put the chocolate carefully into my pocket, I heard a voice. "What are you guys doing? Buying snacks on the way home! Didn't you hear teacher say you shouldn't do that? I'm going to tell on you all!"

It was Etsuko, our class representative, a smug girl who always had a ribbon in her hair and was constantly telling on kids to the teacher.

"Shut up, Etsuko!" I snapped. "If you tell, I'll hit you!"

"If you hit me, I'll tell again!" she replied without a pause.

Toru tried to deal with her next. "Hey Etsuko, what was up with those gym bloomers you were wearing last year? You looked like you were wearing a fat pumpkin! Don't wear those fat pumpkin shorts again!" He made a shape with his arms like a big pumpkin around his waist. Etsuko's face turned red and she looked as if she was about to cry.

"I'm telling the teacher!" she said in an upset voice, then began running towards the school.

"Oh no."

"Let's go home before Kondo gets here."

"Yeah, let's go, let's go."

The four of us walked quickly away, all

the while calling out a checklist of the things we'd need for tomorrow. A lunchbox, gym clothes, a headband, split-toe tabi socks, a flask (I always took my mother's tea with me on Sports Day). As we went through the list, we got faster and faster until we were no longer walking, but running. At some point, we noticed a figure in the distance, then we got closer and closer.

"Isn't that your brother, Mamoru?"

Kenji had recognized Shinichi, although it wasn't difficult to spot him. He wore glasses and he was small for his age—more like a fourth grader than a sixth grader, really. He was also walking along while reading a book, making him look a little like the famous bronze statue of Kinjiro Ninomiya.

"Your brother's such a good student."

"Yeah."

"You're his brother, but you're hopeless in class."

"So what? I'm going to play baseball and join the Giants like Nagashima. Who cares about studying?"

"Hey, he's going to get hit!"

Walking right down the middle of the road and totally engrossed in his book, Shinichi almost bumped into a middle-aged man on a bicycle.

I instinctively closed my eyes. *What a slow poke! Can't he ever take a break from studying? Even if only for the day before Sports Day! Why does he always have to show me up!*

Half-ready to slip away, I opened my eyes slowly.

"Hey, he stepped aside just in time."

"He dodged the bike right as they were about to collide. Perhaps he's actually quite athletic," said Kenji, looking impressed.

"No, no. He's only pretending to read the book," said Toru. "He actually has his eyes on his surroundings, not the book. Isn't that right, Mamoru?"

I almost nodded to agree with Toru's teasing words, but instead I decided to stand up for my brother, saying, "You idiot. My brother's athletic too. He can run faster than you."

"No way!" said Toru, rising to the challenge. "Let me prove it tomorrow. Hey, you guys, don't you think we should find out who's really the fastest?"

Yutaka, who was confident about his running abilities, said yes, but Kenji didn't look very enthusiastic. As for Toru, he didn't say anything more. But that was probably because I was staring him down.

"Hey look," said Kenji, "a dragonfly—no,

two dragonflies. Horny dragonflies! They're stuck together!"

Obviously trying to change the subject, he began chasing the pair of dragonflies. Sure enough, the rest of us joined in and we all began running home.

"Mom, did you buy me a new shirt and shorts?"

We had finished dinner and I wanted to try on my new outfit.

"They're in the bottom drawer with your brother's outfit. Don't take them out now, though," my mother called out from the kitchen over the sounds of washing up, as if she'd read my intentions.

"Okay."

Here they are.

Most of my clothes were hand-me-downs

from my brother, but every year, once a year, for Sports Day, Mom bought me a brand-new set of gym clothes. A pair of white shorts, a white short-sleeved shirt, a pair of tabi socks and on the very top of the pile, a red and white reversible headband folded into a pentagon. Not wanting to take them out right away, I sniffed at their new smell, like a puppy with its nose in a bowl of food.

"What a nice smell," I thought, drinking in the scent of new cotton, veneer drawers and camphor balls.

"What are you doing, you idiot?" my dad said. "You're not going to put those on and go running round the house. Hurry up and go to bed!"

Dad was always scolding me like that, especially when he'd been drinking.

"Shinichi, your kit is here too!" I called out

to my brother, who seemed to be studying at the desk in the corner of the room. But Shinichi didn't respond. Looking at his back, I got the impression he was being stubborn, so I called out to him again.

"Shinichi, come on! Let's try them on and practice our starts. If you practice, you might not come in last tomorrow!"

"Mamoru! Don't make fun of your brother," Mom called out, wiping her hands on her apron. "Your brother is first in his studies, so it doesn't matter if he comes in last at Sports Day. It's smart for him to keep on studying. Running fast isn't going to make you any money in the future!"

My brother had come in last in the races every year, from first grade to fifth. And not only had he come in last, but he'd come in far behind the second slowest person. In fact, there had been times when he'd been so slow that he'd crossed the finish line only moments before the winner of the next race. Our dad, who had shown up drunk, teased him, "Hey Shinichi, it looked like you came in first for a change!" And although deep down I knew that it was great that he did well in class and that it shouldn't matter if he didn't do well on Sports Day, I still felt embarrassed about his performance. Although not as embarrassed as I knew Shinichi felt.

On the morning of the previous year's Sports Day, when I was in the second grade and Shinichi was in the fifth, Shinichi had claimed that he had a stomach ache and therefore needed to stay home from school. The year before that, I'd made him feel bad by showing him the notebook I won for coming first in my race, while he'd come last in his. "Mom, I think Shinichi's trying to skive off school," I'd said. But Mom had slapped me across the head and said the same exact thing: "Your brother comes in top of the class in his studies, so it doesn't matter where he comes in on Sports Day. It's nothing you need to be worried about anyway, so get yourself off to school!"

"Shinichi, I bet you're going to say your stomach hurts tomorrow morning."

"No I won't," said Shinichi, his words coinciding with the sound of Mom slapping me across the head again. Usually, this was where Dad butted in saying, "You idiot, all guys need is to be number one in something, whether it's running or studying. Me, I'm number one when it comes to being a carpenter."

To which Mom would respond, "That's right. Kids, look at this house your father built. It's falling apart."

"How dare you! What gives you the right

to talk like such a hot shot?" Dad would snap back. Then the whole thing would blow up into a quarrel involving the whole family. But not on the night before Sports Day.

Although I gave up on the idea of practicing outside, I did change into my gym clothes and put on my headband and tabi socks. Then I practiced my starts and checked my running form by pretending the space around the table was a track.

"Ready, set, go," I called to myself. "Ready, set, go."

"If you don't stop making such a racket and go off to bed, I won't make you a lunchbox tomorrow!" Mom called.

So with that, I thought it best to go to sleep. Though I never folded my clothes when I took them off, I did that evening, laying my new gym clothes down neatly by my pillow. And I didn't forget to put the chocolate bar next to them, too.

As I lay there in my futon thinking about the next day, I found it impossible to get to sleep. In fact, the more I tried to get to sleep, the less sleepy I felt. Just as I was wondering what to do, Shinichi rustled his way into the futon next to me. I felt like I'd been joined by an old ally, and it made me happy.

"Shinichi, I'm sorry about before," I said.

"It's all right, it didn't bother me," said Shinichi, but his expression was pitiful.

"Shinichi, do you think Airhead will run tomorrow? I wonder if he's still sick."

"Him, huh? I'm sure he'll come. I bet he'll be as fast as always and come in first again."

I felt relieved to hear my brother say that. Then I fell into a deep sleep.

In the morning, I awoke to the smell of my

mother toasting seaweed in the kitchen.

"Mom, is the weather nice?" I shouted.

I'd been thinking about what the weather would be like as I put on my gym clothes. Sports Day just wasn't the same if it wasn't sunny!

"Don't worry, the weather is nice. Now hurry up and go wash your face and eat your breakfast. Everyone else is already heading to school."

"What?!"

According to the plans I had made in my mind when I was lying in bed the night before, I was going to go to school a little early so I could take a few practice runs around the track before the teachers arrived.

"Mom! Why didn't you wake me up earlier? My plans are all messed up now. I told you to wake me up early. You forget so easily."

"Shut up!" boomed my dad, rolling off his

futon and onto the tatami-mat floor.

I rushed through and inhaled my breakfast, continuing to grumble to myself all the while.

"Shinichi, you hurry up too," Mom said. "Leave together with Mamoru."

"I'm fine. I'll leave after Mamoru," he said with a glum expression.

Then I noticed a chocolate bar next to my brother's knees. It was the same as the one I'd bought at Goggle-eyed Gran's the day before. But my chocolate bar was in my back pocket, which meant my brother had bought one too.

Shinichi wants to win too, I thought to myself, he just doesn't want anyone to know.

"What are you saying?" Mom replied to my brother. "I'm going to make you guys a delicious lunchbox and follow you, so you have to go and try your best even if you don't want to."

Urged on by this, Shinichi reluctantly got

ready, and headed off to school with me. All along the way, he looked down dispiritedly while I hopped around him—like an old man walking his dog. By the time we got to the school grounds, kids in brand-new gym clothes were chasing each other and squealing with joy. Others were hanging from exercise bars or practicing the long jump. It seemed as if nobody could conceal their excitement. This was exactly the reason why somebody always got hurt right before Sports Day started.

When Mamoru walked into his classroom, everybody was already there and talking excitedly with flushed faces. Yutaka's excitement was also evident from the way he kept retying his headband and tucking his shirt in his shorts.

"Aren't your pants a little yellow in the front?" Kenji said to Yutaka, who looked down in embarrassment. I quickly checked my shorts too, but there wasn't a single stain on them. A little relieved, I looked at Yutaka's shorts and noticed that there was indeed a yellow stain around the front zipper. Not only that, his shorts looked a little yellow all around.

"I bet you got your pants from your brother, didn't you, Yutaka," said Kenji, and Yutaka dropped his head even further.

"Don't pick on him," said Toru. "Yutaka's in our class relay team. It'll be your fault if he gets distracted and we lose the race. And you know we'll have to all sit on our knees if we lose." Then I noticed that Toru's shirt had a patch on it in the underarm area. It seemed to be made from a beige undershirt, so it was quite clearly visible against the white of his cotton shirt.

"No fighting today," I interrupted, trying to change the subject. "By the way, do you think Airhead will come today? My brother was saying he would come."

Just mentioning Airhead seemed to put everyone in a good mood.

The next moment, some girls who had been looking out the window at the field started laughing out loud.

"What kind of outfit is that? It looks idiotic."

"He's an idiot. A real Airhead."

Airhead had arrived!

Me and the others ran over to the window, pushing the girls aside so we could get a good view. Sure enough, there was Airhead, waddling along like a sumo wrestler. He was so unusually large for a sixth grader, and he was wrapped in the kind of padded kimono you can borrow when you stay at a hot spring inn. Suddenly, he stopped in his tracks and dropped his head so low that he seemed to be looking at the ants on the ground—

all the while, his shoulders were heaving with deep breaths.

"Airhead's wearing a padded kimono!" shouted Kenji.

"He looks really sick. There, look, he's fallen over. I wonder if he's okay?"

"Hey, he's stood up again."

"He looks like he's really forcing himself. Like he's on his final legs," said Toru.

"But I'm glad." I said. "At least he didn't stay home. You might as well have no Sports Day at all if Airhead isn't going to take part. Hey, let's all cheer Airhead on."

So we all stuck our heads out of the window and shouted, "Come on! Come on, Airhead!"

Staggering along down below, Airhead looked up at me and my friends, raised his right hand weakly, nodded…then collapsed in a single movement.

After the entire school had marched into the grounds, the Sports Day events began with the second-grade sprints. The tent to the left of the podium was occupied by the cheerful faces of the principal, vice-principal, and the PTA chairman, while the tent to the right was being used by students and teachers responsible for broadcasts and medical assistance. After each race, the students who came in first, second, and third lined up in front of the podium to receive a prize from the principal. The space on the other side was packed with mothers and other family members who would burst into a huge round of applause whenever a student received a prize.

During the events of the other grades, we were supposed to sit at our assigned spots and watch. But we didn't want to watch a bunch of first-graders running around pushing big balls.

We wanted to go and practice our starts. So off we went behind the school building.

"Mamoru, how do you think Airhead is doing?" Kenji said worriedly. "I wonder if he's going to be okay."

"I went over and looked in on him just a little while ago," I replied. "He was sleeping in the corner of the sixth graders' seats with his padded kimono over him. Even so, he was shivering, so I really don't think he'll be up for it."

"Let's all go and check on him."

"No, Kondo will catch us," Toru said. "By the way, did you see Etsuko's bloomers? She's wearing those big, pumpkin ones again this year."

"Toru, I bet you actually like Etsuko," I said. "You're always going on about Etsuko this, Etsuko that."

In a second Toru shouted "You!" and jumped straight at me, while Yutaka and Kenji just stood there laughing. I realized my comment had hit a nerve.

Mr. Kondo's booming voice surprised us all. "Third graders assemble in front of the entrance gate!"

"Hey! It's our turn!" Yutaka said in a spirited voice.

"Mamoru!" shouted Mr. Kondo, who had obviously just spotted them. "And you boys! What are you doing there? If you don't move yourselves quickly I'm going to disqualify you all!"

"Wow, wow. We better go."

And we all sprinted over to the starting line for the 60-meter dash.

I won my race easily and for the third year in a row. Before I started, I'd put up my hand and waved to my mom over in the parents' section (she'd mouthed back at me to stop messing about and just concentrate on the race). And after I passed the podium, I began to run at full speed. I even noticed a senior member of the PTA pointing at me! Then finally, with only 10 meters left to the finish line, I came straight out in front and took first place! Absolutely everything had gone according to plan. And although I had expected to come in first, I still couldn't contain my excitement, so I tried to rush over to where my mom was sitting.

"No, no. You stay sitting at the finish line until everyone is done," said one of the sixth graders in charge, and I noticed Mom's head drop in the distance.

Yutaka also came in first. Kenji and Toru both came in third, consoling themselves, "We didn't do so bad, we did okay."

Me and Yutaka got notebooks and

certificates for coming in first, and the other two just got certificates for third place. But I guess you could say that they had indeed done "okay" as they had at least gotten something.

After that was all done, the four of us happy campers decided to sit in the very front row and call out at the other students, shouting out taunts at the other guys like, "Run, shorty, run!" or "Roll, fatso, roll. It'll be faster!" But our main target was the girls. Relying on the sound of the crowd to drown out our jeers, we called out one nonsense comment after another: "You're wearing your grandma's bloomers" or "Hey, wide ass!" or "Run backwards! Backwards!"

In particular, we all found Toru's first taunt, "Your mom's balls!" to be extremely funny. Unfortunately Etsuko heard it, too, and she didn't seem to appreciate it the way we did.

"I heard that!" she said. "And if you don't

watch your mouth I'm going to tell Mr. Kondo."

As we'd recently discovered the way Toru felt about Etsuko, it was no surprise to see him fall silent.

Suddenly, the clear sky began to turn cloudy and a cold wind began to blow.

"I wonder if the weather's going to hold up. It better not start raining," said Kenji, looking up at the sky.

"I wonder what happened to Airhead. Perhaps he's gone home," said Toru.

Worried, Mamoru decided to go check on Airhead. But he was nowhere to be found in the sixth graders' seats.

It looks like he's gone home, I thought, which sucks.

Just then, Shinichi called out to me, "Mamoru. What are you doing here?"

"Oh, hi Shinichi, has Airhead gone home?"

"No, he was lying dead here until just a moment ago, but then he started foaming at the mouth, so we had to carry him to sick bay."

"Foaming at the mouth? He's out for sure then."

Part of me wanted to laugh, but I was too concerned about how to break the news to the others.

"The nurse told him to go home, but Airhead just kept mumbling, 'I'm definitely going to run. I'm going to run.' That's some determination," said Shinichi. "If I were him, I'd go home straight away. I guess it's understandable given that running is his only joy. But he really is some guy."

Hearing that, I felt a little relieved. There was still a chance.

"Shinichi, I came in first. I hope you do well too."

"I'm sure I won't."

When it came to himself, Shinichi didn't say much.

"It's almost lunch break," I said, then headed back to the third graders' seats to deliver the latest Airhead news.

The final event of the morning session was the relay for second and third graders. Me and Yutaka put on a spectacular display of our abilities, proving our worth as members of the relay team. The exchange of batons, which was something we'd been worrying about, went smoothly. After the race was over, with a big smile plastered on my face, I went to where Mom was sitting.

"Mom, did you see? Did you see? Why am I such a fast runner?"

"Stop blabbering nonsense, and hurry up

and eat your rice balls. You must be hungry," she said. It made me really happy to see Mom turn to the other mothers and say, "He's a real headache this one—physically fit, but never grows up," without being able to hide her smile.

That was when Shinichi joined us.

"Shinichi, this is the certificate and notebook you get for first place. You should try to get one too."

"Stop being so annoying."

"Mamoru, you be quiet and eat. Your brother isn't feeling very well today. Are you feeling a little better, Shinichi?"

"No, I'm not feeling too well."

I thought to myself, What's going on? Why are they making excuses together like that?

Then Mom turned to the other mothers and said, "This one is a really good student, but his health isn't very good."

I just felt it all seemed so unfair to me, so I stuffed my mouth full of rice balls.

"Shinichi, I know your race is up next, but you don't have to try too hard, so eat as much as you like," Mom said.

Shinichi nodded and began stuffing his face with rice balls just as fast as I was.

Then, right before the afternoon events were about to start, the rain started to fall. It was heavy like a summer evening shower, even though it was already October. I sat there worried sick that the rest of the day might be cancelled, but when I looked at Shinichi I could see him smiling at the puddles.

"What are you smiling about?" I demanded.

"Nothing. It's just a nice shower. Mamoru, do you know the expression to describe this kind of rain?"

"Why would I know that?"

"I'll tell you then. In *rakugo* storytelling they call it 'buckets of rain.' In novels it's 'raining tires' and in poetry it's 'restraining rain.'" Shinichi was speaking with a lot of feeling. He was wearing a cheerful expression that was completely opposite to mine.

"Shinichi, does 'restraining rain' mean rain that stops you from having the races?"

"No, you idiot. 'Restraining rain' means—"

Just as Shinichi was about to give an explanation, the rain suddenly weakened, and within several minutes, the sky was completely clear again. A soft beam of sunlight shone down onto the field. And while I was still worried about Airhead, I was glad that Sports Day hadn't been cut short. I smiled at Shinichi and said, "Shinichi, it looks like we can continue with Sports Day!"

All he said in reply was "Shut up."

BOY

Finally, the time had come for the 80-meter dash, in which both Shinichi and Airhead were scheduled to run. I didn't have any other events myself, so I sat with my mother ready to watch.

Though there were now small puddles all over the field, they didn't seem to pose too much of a problem. And as the Sousa March came blasting out of the loudspeakers, the rain-dampened fields seemed to come back to life. "Now…" came the voice of the broadcast officer over the speakers, "we are going to begin the afternoon's events! First up is the sixth grade 80-meter dash. Please welcome the sixth graders with a warm round of applause."

Everybody turned their eyes to the entrance gate.

"Mom, it's Shinichi! Shinichi! Go Shinichi!"

"I can see. Don't make such a fuss. Just watch quietly," said Mom. But she was also leaning forward and clapping enthusiastically.

Shinichi was in the first group for the 80-meter dash. Airhead would be running three groups after him. The five others in the first group were warming up by jumping up and down or shaking their hands and legs. But all Shinichi did was stare up at the sky.

"Shinichi should warm up. I bet he's still thinking about the rain," I said.

"Be quiet and watch," said Mom, slapping me on my head.

"Ready!"

On the signal of the starter, five kids took the crouching start position, with Shinichi being the last to be ready. It was at that moment that Airhead, still wearing a padded kimono, came waddling over to the start line. Shinichi got back up and stood there looking surprised. I was surprised as well, but more than anything, I was worried about Airhead. Surely he must have been delirious with fever? How could he run?

Airhead, who was now squatting, was helped up by some students and taken back to his place in line.

"Ready!" shouted the starter again.

Shinichi must have given himself over to fate, as he quietly adopted the starting stance.

"Set... Go!"

Five of the kids started off at the same moment, with Shinichi following along a moment later. "Go Shinichi! Go!" I shouted as loud as I could. But it was like water off a duck's back. Shinichi was pumping his arms up and down slowly, in a way that clearly said, "Look, I'm not racing, just participating."

He started out behind the other five, and by

the time they were halfway down the track, he was already about ten meters behind.

"Shinichi is hopeless. The way he's running, people are going to tease me too."

Just as soon as those words had left my mouth, the five in front all slipped on a puddle and fell to the ground in a tangle of arms and legs. Not only that, but they all seemed to be having trouble getting back up.

Mom and me were both surprised, but not as much as Shinichi clearly was. Even from where we were sitting, I could see my brother's eyes spring wide open.

"This is your chance, Shinichi!" I shouted. And right at that moment, I saw him turn into a different person. Gone was the boy plodding along because he had to; here was someone filled with determination, running with all his might, eyes turned upwards, mouth pouted in concentration, cheeks shaking with every stride. It was as if Shinichi had become Airhead. He was going for the win!

"Go Shinichi! Go!" Mom let out a loud cheer that bordered on a scream. She was now standing up and clapping her hands together.

And with this unexpected turn of events, I too was leaning forward and cheering with all my heart for my brother.

Already he was ahead of the five fallen runners with an admirable distance in between.

50 meters.

The others had gotten to their feet but were 10 meters behind Shinichi.

60 meters.

Shinichi flailed his arms and legs like he was drowning. He was still in front.

70 meters.

The others strained to catch Shinichi. He

stuck out his chin, his face bright red.

"Shinichi, Shinichi, Shinichi!"

"Go Shinichi!"

Just 8 meters left.

5 meters left.

He'd never run like this. Never with all his might. His legs were giving out. Getting tangled beneath him. But he kept pushing them on. And he threw his whole body at the line.

Finish!

Mom screamed out loud—but it was a scream of shock.

Shinichi had fallen down, scraping his face along the ground. Instead of making it across the finish line, he'd ended up just 30 centimeters short. Just 30 centimeters too soon!

The five others ran past Shinichi's fallen body. Covered in mud, and with his face buried in the ground, he remained still for a while. Eventually, he got up, and slowly stepped across the finish line with his head hung low.

"That was so close, Mom, wasn't it?" I said, but Mom didn't say anything. Instead she let out a deep sigh.

What had it all been for? Why had he run with all his might? He'd been so close to finishing first—why did he have to come in last? All of these questions and more welled up inside me. But I didn't have much time to think about any of them. Because now, it was Airhead's turn to run.

Even as he stepped up to the starting line, Airhead kept on his padded kimono, which resembled the gown the pro-wrestler Rikidozan wore into the ring. In fact, it was only after the starter had called, "On your mark," that he finally took off the kimono. You could see even from a distance that his legs were all wobbly and I really wondered if he'd be able to last the 80 meters.

As it turned out my worries were well founded. Although the pasty-faced Airhead had started off every bit as spectacularly as the year before, his legs had started to wobble before he'd reached the 20-meter mark (reminding me of the way Dad stands when he's drunk). Then Airhead made an unexpected turn off the track—heading straight toward the PTA tent, collapsing right in front of it, his body stretching out and hitting the ground so hard that I heard it from where I was. There was a pause during which time Airhead didn't move an inch. Then the entire field erupted in a startled roar and medical assistants jumped out of their white tent carrying a stretcher.

Though I hadn't noticed him approaching, Kenji was standing right beside me. "Maybe he's dead," he said, unable to conceal the emotion in his voice.

"He's got guts that Airhead," I said.

I was moved to tears by the sheer strength of Airhead's spirit that pushed his shivering, feverish body along right up to the moment where he'd collapsed. I told myself that I would try to do the same if I had a cold or diarrhoea, if that's what it took to win a race. The thought produced a surge of something in my heart.

"Look at you Mamoru, you're crying," said Kenji, whose eyes were also red.

"Come on Mamoru, Shinichi," said Mom, "It's dinner time, so come and sit down. Good job today, both of you."

I'd been trying to figure out where to put my first-place certificate. Unable to decide, I sat down at the table still holding it.

Dad was already drinking.

"Dad, I came in first. This is the certificate."

"I've already seen it many times. Good for you, though. Now hurry up and eat."

"It wouldn't hurt to congratulate me a little more."

"All right. Well done, Mamoru."

Dad was nice to us that day.

"Shinichi, put your book down, and come over here and eat."

Shinichi hadn't said a word to anyone since coming home. He reluctantly came over and sat at the dinner table. He began moving his chopsticks quietly.

"Shinichi, how did your race go?" Dad asked, but Shinichi remained silent.

"So how did it go, Shinichi?"

"Shinichi was really close to coming in first," I butted in.

"Shut up, Mamoru," said Shinichi, his eyes on the table.

"I see, so you almost came in first, huh."

"The others all fell down, and just as Shinichi was about to finish first he—"

"I said shut up," Shinichi interrupted, still looking down.

"I know you really wanted to win, too." I remembered the Goggle-eyed Gran's chocolate.

"Mamoru, be quiet and eat your food," said Mom, trying to sound angry, but with smiling eyes.

Dad also had a smile on his face as he carried his *sake* cup to his mouth.

"But Shinichi, you really were very close," said Mom in a kind voice.

"So close, so close," I agreed.

Shinichi scratched his head and broke into a shy smile.

"There's still next year, Shinichi. Next year," Dad said encouragingly, and Shinichi continued scratching his head, his face red from embarrassment.

I guessed that he regretted what he'd done. That he was embarrassed about trying so hard when he hadn't ever been meant to win. That he was wondering why the other runners had to fall. I imagined he was thinking that it had been a terrible way for everything to end.

"Shinichi, you really were very close," I said to him one more time.

Shinichi nodded and said, "Yes. I was."

"Shinichi, do you remember your last Sports Day in elementary school? The race where you almost came in first?"

"You're such a mean guy, bringing that up. I think it's time you forgot about that," said my brother, his alcohol-flushed face becoming even redder. He obviously remembered that day, more vividly than I did.

"I wonder what Airhead is doing now? Do you know anything about what happened to him, Shinichi?" I asked, feeling nostalgic. He was just so truly impressive that day. In fact, the first thing that comes to my mind when I think of Sports Day is Airhead in his padded kimono.

"You don't know?" said my brother. "Airhead's the president of a construction firm. They have a four-story office building in front of Kita-Senju station, and apparently they're doing very well."

"Is that right? But I thought Airhead couldn't even write his own name."

I was surprised by what my brother had just told me. Airhead—the fittest and gutsiest guy in school, but the most hopeless when it came to studying—had become the president of a successful company.

My brother laughed out loud.

"Life isn't determined by grades in school. You should know that better than anyone, Mamoru."

"You're right," I said.

I smiled and closed my eyes. Inside I was feeling happy and in my mind's eye I could see Airhead. His legs were wobbling like jello beneath him, but nothing in the world could stop him. He just kept on running, running, running.

Maybe, I thought, I've had a little too much to drink.

Nest of Stars

I ran alongside my brother who was on his bicycle. I was practically dragged along as I gripped the back seat with my hand and I could hear the telescope rattling. I'd always reach the top of the hill just as I began to feel like I couldn't go a single step farther. But on that day, I was able to get there easily—my shoulders rising and falling only slightly with my breathing, and my body starting to feel accustomed to the run through having done it so many times.

"Look over there," said my brother Hideo, pointing to the horizon.

"It's the Big Dipper," I cried.

"That's right," said my brother, nodding with satisfaction.

The spot was our own private astronomical observatory. My brother was the head of it, I was the deputy head, and since we'd moved to Osaka we'd come almost every starlit night.

BOY

My mother, my brother and I had moved to Osaka at the end of August, following Dad's death. And the sky I could see from our new apartment looked just the same as the one we could see from Tokyo—with the city lights getting in the way of the stars.

"The Osaka night is garish," our mom had said that night.

And for some reason, I made a mental connection between the Osaka night sky and the lipstick a friend of my mom was once wearing.

The night sky you could see from the top of the hill, on the other hand, that was the real thing. The Big Dipper, which my brother had pointed out to me on our first night up there, could be seen so vividly, as if it were stamped on the northern sky.

My brother started unloading the 5-centimeter astronomical telescope that we'd secured to the back of the bike. It had been a present from our dad to my brother for his birthday, but my brother always told me, "It belongs to both of us."

The first time I ever saw stars with the telescope was in the summer of my first year in elementary school. My dad and brother had carried the brand-new telescope to a nearby empty lot, and having nothing to carry myself, I just followed along behind them.

"Take a look, Toshio," said my dad, holding me up to the eyepiece. I was just a little uncomfortable as he held me suspended in the air, and I remember him smelling of cigarettes. I could see the moon glowing so large in the round field of vision—so big, in fact, that it almost didn't fit. And I could see little holes on its surface too, like the kind you see on a rice cracker.

"No way," I shrieked, excitedly. I just couldn't believe it was possible to see the moon so clearly. I mean, it was just too far away. I thought it must be some sort of trick, like a piece of paper stuck on the other end of the telescope. I turned to my brother in disbelief. "It's just like the picture in my book," he said happily. And I believed him.

Next, I pointed at a random star and said to my dad, "I want to look at that."

He laughed and adjusted the telescope accordingly.

"This one?" he asked.

Pushing my eye up to the lens, I couldn't see a flaming ball of fire or a star covered in sand like the Sahara Desert as I had imagined. Instead, it looked pretty much the same as when you look at it with the naked eye. Confused, I turned to my dad and found my brother holding his stomach in laughter.

That night, my dad explained how far stars are from Earth and how big they are. He told me that some stars are located many thousands of light years away and that a light year is the distance traveled by light in a year. Imagining light traveling on and on for thousands of years brought the word "infinite" to mind, as it was a word I'd only recently learned. But this wasn't the same "infinite" as in "it would be great to have an infinite amount of potato chips." Thinking about this kind of infinite made my head hurt. An infinite like that was scary, even. So I put my arms around my dad's neck and held on tight.

That was my first encounter with stars. Now that I think about it, I wonder what Mom had been doing that night.

Things were different now, of course. I

learned the names of many constellations from my father and brother, and now I knew how big the galaxy is, too. In fact, I bet I could even use the telescope by myself if my brother wasn't around. That day the two of us had carried the telescope up to the top of the hill to see the Taurus meteor shower. And ten minutes into the climb, the nutmeg leaves that were still wet from the day before's rain had started clinging to my legs, dribbling dew down through my socks and forming small puddles between my toes.

Once we'd reached the summit, my brother assembled the telescope and wanted to train it on Sterope. I opened the *Book of Seasonal Constellations* and turned on the flashlight, learning that Sterope served as the shoulder of Taurus and could be found in the eastern sky at this time of year. So I started to look for Taurus.

I found Taurus immediately, but I struggled

to find the star symbolizing the horn as it overlapped with the Milky Way. I tried to draw a line in the sky, wondering why ancient people had imagined they could see cows and snakes up there. The sky never appeared to me that way. Even when I drew lines between the stars they didn't seem to take on any shape. If I couldn't find the horn for Taurus, maybe we could make do with a female cow for the night.

"I found it." My brother called out, moving aside to let me see.

"How many can you see?"

"One, two, three... Hmm, about fifteen."

I could see about six of the stars of Taurus with the naked eye. So with the telescope, I would be able to see about twenty.

"Wow!" I yelled without moving away from the eyepiece.

I'd seen a shooting star.

BOY

My brother was crouching on the ground, looking up at the sky in silence. Marking the top of the sky was Cassiopeia. I stared at it until the "W" began looking like an "M". I felt my body being relieved of its weight; I was suddenly overwhelmed by a feeling that we were the only two people left in the universe.

For some reason the school I had just transferred to suddenly came to my mind. I thought of how I had come from Tokyo. How the words I used were different. How everybody made fun of everything I did, calling me "Tokyo." The kids at my new school seemed to have a problem with everything about me.

"Toshio, have you made friends at school?" my brother asked me suddenly.

I tried to say "yeah" but the question had startled me, and the word got stuck in my throat. Tears welled up in my eyes.

"Are they picking on you?" my brother asked.

I snuffled my nose, but somehow managed to say, "No, no." But this just made more tears roll down my face.

"You'll make friends soon enough. You have to try to fit in. Isn't there anyone you click with? Like someone that likes to look at stars? You could take the telescope to school with you. Show your new friends. Tell them all the things you know about stars," he said. "I've already been asked if I'd like to be the head of the astronomy club at school when I become a third year student!" he added with a laugh.

"Head of the astronomy club! That's so cool!" I gasped, and immediately my tears stopped flowing.

"You know, it's almost the season for Sirius."

"Sirius. Yeah."

I knew all about Sirius. It appears in the eastern sky. The Arabs in the desert called it "the star of a thousand colors" because it changes color right before your eyes, going from blue to white, to green, then purple. Just like a kaleidoscope.

"Sirius is the brightest star, isn't it?"

"That's right," said my brother. "Its diameter is only twice the sun's and its distance from earth is 8.6 light years, so it's the closest out of all the fixed stars visible from Japan. That's why it appears the brightest."

My brother's compelling manner of speech was just like my dad's.

"8.6 light years, huh?"

Eight years ago Dad had still been alive. So the light that left Sirius then was only just about to reach Earth. Allowing us to see light from the past like that, space can be like a giant photo album. The thought made me feel that we hadn't been left forgotten at the edge of space—a thought that helped me regain my courage.

We were now in the season in which Sirius exuded a cold, bright glow.

Osaka was cold too. I was waiting for my brother after school at the Lawson convenience store. It was already fifteen minutes later than the time we'd agreed to meet, but he still hadn't shown. I always waited there for him on days when Mom needed to work late. We'd buy our dinner there and eat it along with a salad Mom had left for us. That was what she'd asked us to do soon after we'd moved to Osaka.

Mom worked as a designer, and she often returned home after we'd gone to bed. Sometimes she would cry in the middle of the night and, at other times, she would spend a long time on the phone. I knew she used to cry sometimes when my dad was alive too, so it couldn't have been because Dad died. I wondered why she cried. Perhaps like me, she was being bullied at her work. But I didn't like the phone calls at night because I could sense a man on the other end of the phone.

Anyway, back to my brother who was now really late. As I waited for him, I thought of how I might get the *oden* hotpotch for dinner. I could maybe even get the latest copy of *Jump Comic*. I was walking towards the magazine rack when I saw someone I didn't want to see. Fat-Ken. He was always carrying a Hanshin Tigers baseball megaphone with him and wearing the team's pinstriped kit with the girly name "MAYUMI" (it was the surname of a player, but written in English it sounded like the first name of a girl) emblazoned across the back. He always wore really girly jeans, too.

I'd already been bullied by him at school that day, so I hid behind the magazine shelves to avoid him. Fat-Ken had a few cronies, including a guy called Hitoshi. Basically, these guys were like a backing chorus for him. His cronies would chirp "that's impressive" when Fat-Ken boasted about how his dad had built all seven of the Pachinko gambling houses in the city, and respond "that's right" to something or other Fat-Ken said with his bottom lip sticking out.

That was actually the day I was supposed to become one of the popular kids in class—the day I did as my brother suggested, to show everyone how cool I was, through my knowledge of stars. I'd seen an opportunity to do this after lunch break when Fat-Ken happened to bring up the subject of stars.

"Hey Tokyo!" he called out, "I hear you spend all your free time looking at stars!"

Someone must have told Fat-Ken about how I went to the top of the hill almost every night. That made things simple, though. In fact, it was the chance I'd been waiting for, so in one breath I told them what my brother had taught me about Sirius.

Then I fixed a firm gaze on Fat-Ken. I said in my heart, What do you think of that, huh?

"Hah, whatever. Everyone knows that," he blurted out smugly. "But did you know that Sirius is a double star?"

"A double star?" I parroted. I'd never heard of such a thing.

"So you don't even know about double stars? Stupid Tokyo. I thought you had a telescope!"

"Maybe he's been using a magnifying

glass," piped up one of his gang.

"Of course I've got a telescope!" I shouted, unable to keep my voice down.

"How big is it?" Fat-Ken asked right away.

"5 centimeters."

"5 centimeters? That's just a toy!" Fat-Ken said triumphantly.

"5 centimeters, he says, 5!" repeated his backing chorus of cronies.

I felt like they were making fun of both my dad and my brother.

"Ask your dad to buy you a bigger one!" they added.

It was then that Satomi Suzuki spoke up. "That's so mean. You know his dad died."

Her blue mini-skirt swayed.

Everyone fell silent for a moment. But Fat-Ken broke the silence by cupping his hands like a megaphone in front of his mouth and hectoring,

"5 cm! 5 cm!"

I wish you were dead, I thought to myself; and I so much wanted to beat him up. But I couldn't move. I just made a tight fist instead. And from then, right up until the last class of the day, every time they saw me Fat-Ken's group taunted, "5 cm! 5 cm!" while I did my best to keep my eyes on the floor.

Fat-Ken bought a couple of comic books and left the store. Then just as I was thinking that I shouldn't come to the store anymore, my brother walked in. Seeing his face almost made me cry, but I held in my tears and stared at the cover of *Jump Comic* instead.

The walk back home with my brother felt longer than usual. It was just the two of us for dinner as always, but neither of us said much. Normally my brother would ask me what the matter was if he sensed I was quiet, but that night he stayed silent too. Perhaps he'd had a bad day as well.

After dinner, I put the plates in the sink and poured washing-up liquid over them. Then I threw away the salad in a plastic bag kept in the corner of the sink. A piece of celery missed the bag and fell onto the sink and I noticed that both ends of it were neatly sliced. Quickly I took the salad back out of the plastic bag and ate it all as quickly as possible. Maybe not just for my mom who'd made it for me, but for Dad, too.

After that, I walked into the "Nest of Stars." That was the name I'd given to our room. My brother was already lying on the bottom bunk of our bed staring at the ceiling of constellations we'd made from pins coated in fluorescent paint. When the lights went off, the pins glowed, making it look like a microcosm, with Queen Cassiopeia, the Big Bear, and the Small Bear.

My brother got up.

"So how did your talk about stars go? Did you tell your friends about them?"

I told him the truth. "There was a guy with an 8-centimeter telescope."

"I see. An 8-centimeter, huh."

My brother pulled the string of the fluorescent light, bringing the room back into day. Then he pulled it again, bringing back the night. He kept doing this over and over, on, off, on, off. Day, night, day, night. The he pulled the cord again and left us bathed in light.

"Now what if we had a 10-centimeter?" he said. "Then we could even see the companion star of Sirius. It would be so much better than an 8-centimeter. That's what we'll do! We'll buy ourselves a 10-centimeter, take a photo of the

Sirius companion star and see what they have to say about that!"

"You say we'll buy one but…" I started. On seeing my brother's expression, I hastened to say, "I have 5,000 yen that grandpa in Nara gave us and 4,000 yen I saved from my pocket money in my bear coin bank."

"And I have 300,000 yen, so we should have enough."

"300,000 yen?!"

Why did he have that much money? When and how had he saved so much? I stared at my brother, but he avoided eye contact with me and instead turned his gaze to our father's 5-centimeter telescope standing by the wall. I also turned to look at it and I felt a little guilty, like we were betraying Dad by buying a new telescope.

"I'm home!"

It was Mom calling out from the front door,

followed by the sound of dragging slippers approaching our room.

"Did you guys eat the salad?"

It was the first thing she always asked us on coming home. Her next words were always, "I'm exhausted. You guys go to sleep." We were always saying those words in our minds before she actually said them.

"There's somewhere the three of us are going to go next Sunday, okay?" Mom said, sounding like a school teacher. This was unexpected news. There was something sweet about the breath from her lipstick-smeared lips, and I held my breath. My brother didn't say anything either. He just lay down on his bed and closed his eyes.

Usually I dozed off before the pin stars lost their glow, but that night I just couldn't get to sleep. It seemed like my brother couldn't fall asleep either as I could hear him tossing and turning on the bottom bunk. I picked up a book from my brother's bookshelf, *A Tour of the Constellations*, and got back into bed with it, suddenly remembering the double stars Fat-Ken had mentioned.

According to the book, double stars were also called binary stars. And when I looked up the section on Sirius, it said that Sirius was a binary star and that its companion star was a rare white dwarf star. A White Dwarf? There was something sinister about that name!

I kept on reading and found out that the companion star had a diameter only three times as large as Earth's but that its mass was 250,000 times as large. As a result, a matchbox would weigh 2 tons and a human being 2,600 tons on the star.

2,600 tons? I couldn't even imagine how

heavy that was! I raised my hand to feel its weight, thinking how the creatures on the companion star would have a tough time doing the same. What would they do when they wanted to jump up? Surely Fat-Ken would weigh at least 3,000 tons there. And with these thoughts in my mind, I dozed off to sleep.

When I walked into my classroom the next day, there was a circle of kids around Fat-Ken as usual. I tried to sit down without meeting his eyes, but I could hear him saying, "This is an 8-centimeter, an 8-centimeter. Any smaller and you can't see anything."

I couldn't help myself from turning my eyes towards the voice, and through a crack in the circle of people, I saw a shiny white, thick tube. It was an 8-centimeter telescope. Fat-Ken had brought it all the way to school just to show off.

"This is amazing. It makes a 5-centimeter look like a pencil. No, more like a toothpick," said one of his merry men. The others nodded in agreement and they all looked over at me. I just left the classroom without saying anything. Their laughter chased after me into the hall. And by the time I left the school gates, I was running. Faster, faster. Up to the hill. To me and my brother's celestial observatory.

My legs carrying me onward and upward, I reached the top of the hill without stopping once. The sky went round and round with each breath. My chest was beating heavily. And even after I'd closed my eyes and lain down on the ground, I felt like I was still running.

That night, Mom was cooking in the kitchen for the first time in a while. She was making soup and fried shrimp. The meal tasted good, but I was worried about the bruise and swelling on my brother's cheek. But before I could even ask him about it, he explained that he had fallen. Mom didn't seem to even notice. She was always preoccupied these days.

After we finished eating, Mom said, "There's someone I'd like you both to meet this Sunday. I like him, so I'm sure you'll like him too."

When I asked, "Is it a man?" my brother quickly said with a stern face, "Of course it is."

I went back to our "Nest of Stars." I tried to say something to my brother, but he kept staring up at the ceiling in silence, so I couldn't find the right moment.

"Our next dad—" I started to say, then quickly corrected myself, "the guy we're going to see soon. Why don't we get him to buy us a 10-centimeter telescope? In exchange for Mom,

I mean."

I looked into my brother's face.

"Don't be stupid. How can we let someone who isn't even our dad buy us something like that. *I'll* buy us the 10-centimeter."

I regretted my careless remark. What an ass I was.

But still, I wondered, how could Mom forget about Dad so quickly? It was Dad that had taught us about constellations, and it was also Dad who had taught us how to make a fire without using matches or a lighter. Hadn't Mom ever heard Dad talk about the stars? Did adults forget everything so quickly?

On Sunday, my brother and I were made to wear matching jackets and leather shoes and we followed Mom, looking like the close-knit family of spot-billed ducks in central Tokyo that was

on TV a lot. Christmas music was already play-
ing in town.

"I wonder where we're going?" I said to my
brother.

"We're going to go eat with the man," he
answered, sounding bored.

"Let's not," I said, quietly enough so that
Mom couldn't hear. But my brother didn't
respond. We were walking so slow that Mom
turned around and said, "Come on guys, walk
faster." But her voice was surprisingly kind.

Mom always tied her hair up, but today she
had it down like young women do. Before leaving
the house, she kept looking in the mirror and
powdering her nose.

We were going to have lunch at a place
inside the Marunouchi Building. We went up to
a restaurant on the top floor with a view. A man
in a bow tie came over to our mom, the two of

them exchanged some words, and he signaled towards the window with his right hand. We turned to look in the direction he was indicating, and a man in a gray suit, wire glasses, and a thin mustache stood up and bowed.

So this was the kind of guy Mom liked? He looked very different from Dad, who always used to wear ripped jeans on weekends.

"Let me introduce you to Mr. Fujita. He works as a designer at the same company as me. This is Hideo, he's a second year in junior high, and Toshio is in the fourth grade."

"It's nice to meet you both," said the man with a shy smile.

I got the feeling that he might be a nice person. But if he was a nice person, then I felt sorry for my dead dad. I mean, that would mean...I shot a glance at my brother, but he still had his eyes on the floor.

"Come on now," said my mom, after a moment of silence.

Still looking down, my brother said, "Hello." I quickly said "Hello" too and bowed.

"Where are your manners? Can't you even say your greetings properly?" Mom said.

"It's okay, it's okay. They're both a little shy because it's the first time we're meeting. I'm the same way. Why don't we just sit down and get something to eat."

I didn't mind his version of the Osaka dialect. It really depended on the person using it. It sounded better than when Fat-Ken used it, that was for sure.

"Now, what should we have?"

The man handed us the menus.

"I'll look for you guys," said Mom, taking the menu away from me, and decided on cream soup, hamburger steak and rice, and salad without bothering to ask us.

"That'll be fine for both of them," she said.

It was fine with me. And my brother didn't seem to really care.

"I'll have the onion gratin soup, mushroom salad, and the sole cooked in wine," continued Mom. She was in high spirits. As for the man, he said his stomach was hurting, so he just ordered some wine and cheese.

During the meal, it seemed like Mom was doing all the talking and the man was just smiling and listening to her. When Dad was alive, he had been the one who was always talking to Mom, and her role had been to nod and listen. It seemed like it was the total opposite with this person. Every so often, the man would try to include us in the conversation by asking us things like what subjects we liked in school and what sports we were good at. I would try to say something, but before I could, Mom would answer him.

After what felt like a very long meal ended, the four of us stepped out of the Marunouchi Building.

"I have something to go do with Mr. Fujita now, so you two go straight on home, okay?" Mom said.

We did as we were told and walked across the zebra crossing towards the nearest station. Mom and the man waved at us. Suddenly I didn't like him anymore. It felt like completely different things: Mom and Dad standing next to each other, and Mom and that man standing next to each other.

After getting off the train, we waited at the bus stop in front of the station. Since it was Sunday, there was a bus only every thirty minutes or so. We lived in such an inconvenient place! My brother was reading his *Pocket Encyclopedia of Constellations* and I killed time by swinging around the pole that marked the bus stop. The only other person waiting for a bus was a middle-aged man.

"Hey, one-man constellation club!"

I turned around to see four junior high students surrounding my brother. When my brother didn't say anything, one of them stepped forward.

"Stars? Again? What are you thinking making a constellation club? How dare you make a new club without even asking anyone! Nobody wants to join your club anyway! Nobody cares about stars! Why don't you study something else, you idiot? Then maybe you wouldn't get an 'F' in math, P.E., social studies and everything else! You don't know about anything else, do you?

You're just a star freak!"

I was shocked. I'd thought he was popular in his class. I'd thought he was going to be the head of the constellation club.

One of them turned to me. "You the younger brother of this idiot?"

"Leave us alone!" shouted my brother.

"What the..." Suddenly, the tall one hit my brother. Then the others joined in hitting him too, but he didn't fight back. They knocked him to the ground and he began to cry. Then I felt my knees go weak and I began to cry too.

"Hey, stop it! Hey!" yelled the man sitting at the bus stop.

And the group ran away into the station.

"What terrible kids. Are you okay?" asked the man, helping my brother to his feet. "Your new clothes are all dirty," he added, dusting my brother's clothes off. And I helped do the same.

Still crying, my brother began walking off without saying a word to me or the man. Apparently he was going to walk all the way home. I tried hard to keep up with him so I wouldn't get lost and by the time we got home it was already dark. All the while my brother hadn't said a single word. But at least he'd stopped crying.

When we got inside, he immediately shut himself up in the "Nest of Stars," slamming the door shut as if to say, "Leave me alone, I don't want to talk to you." I wasn't sure what to do. Not only was my brother being bullied at school, but he was being bullied worse than me. And even though he was having such a hard time, he'd been trying hard to cheer me up.

I plucked up the courage to walk into our room and found him reading the *Encyclopedia of Constellations* with puffy eyes. I felt a little relieved.

BOY

"Should we go buy a 10-centimeter telescope and go look at the companion star of Sirius?" I asked. I thought that it might cheer my brother up if we did. Stars were the only thing that we could rely on now. And I thought our dead dad would have probably agreed.

My brother gave a dry response. "We don't have the money."

"We have more than 300,000 yen."

"That was a lie. I only have about 50,000 yen."

So that was a lie too? First the lie about becoming head of the constellation club. Now the 300,000 yen. What was I supposed to do?

"Let's leave," my brother said looking into my eyes. And the thought made me happy, although I didn't really know why, so I said, "Yes."

"You know, there's a 10-cm telescope in the

science lab of my junior high. Let's borrow that and go look at Sirius."

He was back to being my usual, dependable big brother.

"Will they let you borrow it?"

"They won't know if we return it straight after. You know, by now we should be able to see Sirius right under Orion."

"If we return the telescope right away, then it's not stealing, right?"

"Exactly. Now, let's go before Mom comes home. Today's Sunday so there'll be nobody at school. Even if there is, it'll only be the janitor."

"What should we tell Mom?"

"We can tell her we went up to the hill to see the stars. And from now on stop saying 'Mom, Mom' about everything. Mom has her own life, and we have ours," my brother said firmly.

BOY

My brother put on a navy jumper and yellow muffler over his sweater and I wore a sweater and my favorite red down vest. We would be prepared no matter how cold it was.

I put my hand on the 5-cm telescope.

"We can leave that. We'll have the 10-centimeter," said my brother, but I really wanted to take it along. I was sure that Dad would want to come with us and my brother didn't object a second time.

We tied the telescope to the backseat of the bike as always, and I ran alongside the bike while keeping a hand on the telescope. The cold made my ears burn. But after running a while my body began to warm up.

"Do you want to change?" my brother said.

He got off the bike, so I rode it and he ran alongside. But because the telescope and my brother's hand were on the backseat, I had trouble keeping my balance and moving straight. My brother's thigh kept hitting the side of the bike too. I looked up and saw Sirius shining brightly in the southeastern sky. It looked as if it were beckoning us to come closer.

When we got to the gates of his junior high, my brother said, "Wait here." I didn't like having to wait alone, but it was easier than having to go into the school.

My brother was going back and forth around the gates trying to find a way to get in. Then he suddenly jumped onto them. They were made of iron, and it was easy for him to climb up and jump over. Suddenly, his face appeared on the other side as he began to unlock the gates. Then he opened them slightly, turned, and disappeared into the school building on the other side of the field without a word.

It felt like a really long time had passed. I

thought about how the science lab was home to things like skeletons, human models, and snakes stored in formalin. Wasn't my brother afraid to go into such a place in the dark? I was glad that I'd waited outside.

Suddenly, a light went on in the second floor, followed by the sound of an alarm inside the school building. He'd been caught! What should I do, I wondered. Should I take the bike and run away? My brother had been caught—or so I thought. The very next moment, a dark shadow carrying a thick tube came staggering towards me. It was my brother. He hadn't been caught, after all. His eyes were wide open and he was breathing heavily. I was so glad that I couldn't help myself calling out to him.

"Hurry up and get on the bike and get moving. To the usual place on the hill!" he shouted back, still running and with his legs all wobbly.

I did as I was told and began pedaling the bike as fast as I could. With the 5-centimeter telescope tied to the backseat, I had trouble keeping the handlebars straight. But I still pedaled with all my strength; I lifted my backside off the seat and pedaled as hard as I could. I remember going along the back of the school, but I don't remember what path I took after that. What was important was that I made it to our usual spot on the hill, though I was drenched in sweat underneath my sweater.

It was only after I reached the hill that I turned around for the first time. My brother had been behind me part of the way, but he was no longer in sight. He probably couldn't run fast enough and had been caught. I suddenly became really worried. I was completely alone. What was I supposed to do from now on?

BOY

"What should I do, Hideo?" I said out loud in desperation, and tears began streaming down my face. If only Dad were here. If only he were still alive.

It was just as I crouched down on the ground that I heard a shout that was actually more like a groan.

"Toshio!" came the voice, followed by heavy breathing. It was my brother. My brother! And he hadn't been caught. He was carrying a big telescope in his arms.

"Hideo!" I shouted and ran to him.

Still breathing heavily with his shoulders, my brother said quickly, "When I opened the glass door with the telescope in it, the alarm went off. I almost succeeded, but when I left the building the janitor saw my face. So I'm done for. I can't go home. Now it's only a matter of time before they find us here. We need to run away somewhere!"

"But, running away, I mean..." I said, trying to plead with him.

"We'll go somewhere with a good view of the stars. We'll go there and look at Sirius." "We have 60,000 yen, so let's get a taxi." "We can't use a taxi. The police will send a report to their radios immediately. We should go to Rokko."

He was asking and answering his own questions and I wondered if he was starting to feel alone.

"But Rokko is far," I said. "I wonder just how far it is from here."

"It's far but it's bikeable. We can get there by midnight."

I did as my brother told me, unloading the 5-centimeter and tying the 10-centimeter to the back of the bike. Its weight lifted up the front wheel of the bike slightly.

"Toshio, you ride the bike. I'll hold it and run."

Even after I sat down on the saddle, it felt like the front wheel would come off the ground with the weight of the telescope. I leaned forward and pedaled with all my strength. My brother ran carrying the 5-centimeter in one arm and holding the 10-centimeter down on the bike with the other. It was a little funny, like the "shopping races" at Sports Day. But I could see my brother's serious expression, so I pedaled with all my might. And as I did, I somehow got the feeling that Dad was running with us.

Soon after we'd started out, we borrowed a second bike without asking the owner. We figured that it would be impossible for my brother to go all the way to Rokko on foot, so we had chosen the oldest looking bicycle from a parking lot of a large apartment complex. Just as we finished tying the 5-centimeter telescope to the backseat and I was about to ride it out of the parking lot, someone said, "Where are you guys going?"

Thinking we'd been rumbled, we turned around very slowly to see a taxi stopped in the street and the driver eyeing us suspiciously.

"We're going to go look at stars," said my brother, his voice quivering. I nodded too.

"Is that right? You're a good brother. Where are you going?"

"To Rokko," I said.

"Rokko? That's a long way from here. At least 20 km. Guess you're going to be an astronomer one day, eh, big brother? Take care then," said the driver kindly, glancing at the 10-centimeter. Looking happy, my brother bowed his head.

After the taxi had disappeared from sight, I

sighed, "That was a close one, wasn't it."

"We'll be fine," my brother assured me. "I mean, we really are going to go look at the stars. Now let's raise our spirits and set off." And with that, he patted me on the shoulder.

Perhaps we had been biking for about an hour when we began seeing signs saying "To Rokko." That was when I started to feel very thirsty. We bought two cans each of coffee and orange juice from a roadside vending machine and downed them. Then I started to feel very worried.

"We're going to go look at Sirius, right?"

"Of course," my brother responded immediately.

"What are we going to do after we look at Sirius? Are we going home? Or are we going to go somewhere far away?"

There was no response. Still squatting on

the ground, my brother was staring into the distance.

"What are we going to do? Say something, Hideo." I was on the verge of tears.

"Toshio."

"Yes."

"From now on each one of us has to live our own lives, relying just on ourselves. Do you understand? Mom will do what she wants to do. I'm also going to go my own way. So even though you're only in fourth grade, and you're still little, you have to live your own life. That's why we're going to first go look at Sirius. We have to go see it. It's the star our dad must have looked at too. Do you understand?"

I didn't understand at all. But if my brother said so, I thought it must be the right thing to do. I was already tired, and all I really wanted to do was find somewhere warm to go to sleep. But we were going to go look at Sirius, so sleep could wait.

"We're almost there now, so let's cheer up and go. We'll get another coffee along the way, if you like," my brother said, gripping the handlebars of his bike.

After riding for another twenty minutes, we came to an upward slope. We were already struggling on a flat road, so going uphill was really tough. We took frequent breaks, and every time we did, I wanted to say, "Let's go home Hideo, Mom'll be worried," but when I saw my brother's serious face, I couldn't say anything.

Halfway up the hill we decided to get off and push our bikes. I pushed my bike with all my strength so that I wouldn't fall behind.

"We're almost there," my brother called out. "Just a little farther to the observation platform."

Maybe it was just a little more, but it felt like forever. Then just as my hands pushing the bike were starting to go numb along with my ankles, the big sky presented itself before us.

I wanted to yell "We're here!" but I'd lost my voice. My brother must have felt the same way; he looked at me with a small grin.

The important thing was that we had made it. We didn't have to push the bikes any further. I wanted to sit down for just a little while. But I felt like if I sat down once, I wouldn't be able to get up again, so I stayed standing and looked up at the sky. It was so full of stars. Winter stars that were glowing, so sharp and bright. I felt like they were penetrating my eyes and I wondered why. Then there, among the countless stars was Sirius—larger, and shining more brightly than all the others. It was the king of the universe.

My brother took the 10-centimeter telescope off the back of the bike and began to set it up very slowly. I tried to help him, but my hands were numb and hurting from the cold, so I could not touch anything. He was using what energy he had left to set up the tripod and shuffling his feet to keep warm. But, just like me, his hands weren't working properly and he kept dropping parts on the ground.

Finally, the 10-centimeter was all set up, although it did look a little top-heavy and unstable sitting there on the tripod built for the 5-centimeter.

"It's ready," said my brother, turning to face me, his face like that of a ghost in the glare of my flashlight. A ghost that was freezing to death, anyway. I'm sure my face probably looked the same.

We both ran in place to keep warm as we

pointed the telescope at Sirius with our numb hands. Then we set the polar axis on the North Star and the declination axis on Sirius. Minus 16 degrees, 42 minutes, 58 seconds.

"Wow," cried out my brother. Then he turned to me and nodded. I took my brother's place and looked into the eyepiece.

"I see it!" I shouted, forgetting the cold, my fatigue and my worries.

Blue, white, green, purple, red. The Arabs were right! It really was "the star of a thousand colors." I was so happy I'd managed to see what I wanted. That it had all worked out.

"The companion star," said my brother.

I strained my eyes and to my amazement, I saw a dot shining white next to the color-changing Sirius. It was a smaller star that looked like it was hiding. So this was the White Dwarf star, with a mass 250,000 times that of Earth.

BOY

"It's there, it's there!"

I waved for my brother to come and change places with me, but he just crouched down behind me and said, "I'm okay, as long as you've seen it." And that's where he stayed.

After a while, it started snowing. The first snow of the winter. Delicate flakes of white covered my brother's head and shoulders and there was a thin layer of snow on his yellow muffler too. By then, my hands and feet weren't hurting anymore. But my body wouldn't move the way I wanted it to.

Then I remembered one thing more I needed to do: to show the companion star to Dad's telescope! Even if it was only a 5-centimeter, it was still Dad's telescope, and I was sure it would be able to capture it.

I brushed the thin layer of snow off Dad's telescope, then set it to Sirius, dragging my heavy body, arms and legs. Clouds began filling up the sky and it was only a matter of time before they obscured the view. I needed to hurry, hurry, hurry. But my sluggish body wasn't listening to me properly.

Then, there it was. I could see Sirius in the sky. It had changed its position to the edge of a mountain, showing just how much time had passed since we'd arrived. I looked down into the eyepiece.

And I saw it! But what? Why was it so blurry? Maybe snow had gotten in the way. Or maybe even my tears.

The Sirius I saw with my blurry vision was a vague white dot. But I thought I saw Sirius and its companion star.

It was enough. I was glad. I'd done what I had to do—what my brother had told me to do. Now I could live on my own.

BOY

I walked over to where my brother was crouching, now with snow dusting his head and clothes.

I'm squatting, too. I may squat now, right, Hideo?

I gazed back to look at the southeastern sky. Sirius had already hidden itself behind the clouds.

Okamesan

Takoyakushi Street in Chukyo Ward. Turn east off Tomino Lane. Minamoto Inn.

The man at the Kyoto station tourist office had jotted down the directions for him. And with the piece of paper grasped tightly in his hand, Ichiro stood at the front of the entrance to the inn feeling a slight rush of excitement. The word "Minamoto" was painted in brushstrokes on the square paper lantern above the lattice. The lantern was clearly yellowed with age, but Ichiro felt like it was the "authentic Kyoto color," so it brought a smile to his face.

It was the first time for him to travel alone. And it was the first time for him to stay at an inn, so he wasn't quite sure what to say when he walked in. Maybe they wouldn't take him seriously if he said a simple "hello" like a student, but something like "pardon me," on the other hand, could seem a little pretentious. Perhaps he should go all out and say something in Kyoto dialect? All these choices flitted through his head as he waited just inside the entrance.

"What can I do for you, young man?"

A middle-aged woman appeared through the curtains behind the reception desk. She was wearing a worn-out dress and had her gray-streaked hair tied up in a bun. Ichiro had been expecting someone in a kimono, so she took him a little by surprise.

"Is there something I can do for you?" she asked again in an accent that was soft Kyoto, but with a hint of firmness at its core.

"Um, I came to stay here, from Tokyo, for two nights, I'm a student," babbled the usually articulate Ichiro.

"But you're still a child. Did you run away from home or something?"

The phrase "run away from home" pierced

his chest.

"I think it would be best if you hurry on home."

Having said what she needed to say, the woman tried to return behind the curtain. But Ichiro quickly held out his memo.

"Wait! Please wait. Please take a look at this."

He couldn't turn back here. How was he supposed to go sightseeing if he couldn't even find a place to stay?

"What is it?"

She took the memo with leathery hands, toughened most likely from years of work in the kitchen.

"Oh, this is Mr. Okada's handwriting. From the station," she said. "So you really are a customer, after all."

"Yes, I am." He nodded with enough vigor

to make his head fall off. "I came to do research on Kyoto. I'm a high school student from Tokyo and I'm interested in history."

"Research?" She looked at Ichiro as if looking at something strange.

Here we go again, thought Ichiro. The same thing had happened at the tourist center. They took him for a runaway child and wouldn't believe his story about coming to do research on Kyoto. In fact, even after half an hour of explaining, they still didn't believe him and had only introduced the inn after he'd told them the name of the high school. He couldn't help but feel a little proud that K School was known as far afield as Kyoto, but at the same time he also found it annoying. Still, he felt he had no choice but to use the same strategy.

"Yes, I belong to the History Club at K High School, and I've come to see the ancient temples." He raised his voice to emphasize the name of the high school, but the woman didn't appear even remotely impressed. Then, just as he started to feel that the tactic might not work with this woman, she asked him with a suspicious look, "Are you really in high school?"

The question took Ichiro by surprise and he wasn't able to respond immediately.

"Oh well, I guess it's okay. After all, you do have an introduction from Mr. Okada."

Perhaps it was because of her Kyoto dialect, Ichiro couldn't quite tell if the woman had taken a liking to him or not. Relieved, he bowed and said, "Thank you very much."

But she'd already turned her back to him.

The room he was taken to was appalling. True, it only cost 3,500 yen a night, but nevertheless no meals were included and it was evident even to a secondary school student such as himself that this room, with just one small window, an old television and a small table, was really unusually shabby.

There was something that resembled a raised *tokonoma* alcove to his left, and a picture of a Dharma doll hung there, looking as if it had once had water spilled on it, leaving it with oozing eyes that seemed a little eerie. Altogether the room had succeeded in looking old, but failed miserably in feeling traditional. Surely this was much too dreary a place in which to spend his first night in Kyoto.

"I shouldn't have come here," he said to himself. Then, pulling himself together, he tried to think about what to do next. There were temples waiting to be seen, and journeys were all about overcoming difficulties. Now was no time to lose faith. He should push on with determination and seek out the wonderful encounters ahead.

Suddenly he felt thirsty. There wasn't even a glass in the room. He thought about asking the lady for a coke, then decided against it as he didn't want to deal with her prying. Instead, he decided to take a stroll around the Higashiyama area. After all, for a student, a room should be nothing more than a place to sleep.

He picked up his small bag and was about to leave the room when suddenly his eyes fell on what looked like a travel guide on top of the television. Thinking it might come in handy, he picked it up and read it. But it wasn't a travel guide at all. No, it was actually a leaflet advertising a pornographic movie service—a smiling woman on the cover pushing her breasts up at him with her hands. Feeling suddenly flustered, he looked away. But only momentarily. He could not help smiling at her in return.

Though it was free to watch regular TV, he'd have to put 300 yen in the box to see the lady. He felt no hesitation about spending the money. After all, watching a porno film was a fitting experience for a journey. Traveling was about encounters. At once, he slipped the money in the coin box and a small red lamp on top came on. Ichiro adjusted the knob to Channel 2, just in time for the beginning, as the title appeared:

"'Please Do Me': The Neighbor's Wife Series."

Shocked, Ichiro immediately switched off the TV. Yet, uttering out loud, to no one in particular, the excuse that he didn't want to be wasting money, he switched the set back on.

Onscreen, he saw the back of a woman walking through a bamboo forest in what looked like Sagano. She was wearing a kimono. Hey, this is the perfect video for me, Ichiro thought. Unable to control his excitement, he sat just 50 cm from the TV and craned his neck forward to bring his face even closer to the screen. He couldn't help gulping, and murmured, "This woman will be doing kinky stuff?"

"I've brought your tea," the lady's voice came from the other side of the paper sliding door.

No. No. No.

Ichiro turned off the TV in a flash and sat bolt upright with his legs folded under him. With the same disinterested expression on her face, the lady placed a pot and other tea utensils on the table.

"I assume you'll be eating out," she said, looking up at Ichiro's face.

"Y-yes," he rasped.

Looking perplexed for a second, she glanced

at the TV set.

"Oh," she said, suddenly sounding younger. She'd noticed the red lamp on top of the television. Studying Ichiro's face, she grinned. "It's not healthy for a young man like you to be watching that kind of thing all by yourself."

His whole face went bright red. So did the tips of his earlobes. He hung his head and managed a resigned "yes" in a voice no louder than a mosquito's buzz.

"I'm going to Chion-in," he said hurriedly and rushed out of Minamoto Inn as if he were being chased by something. So quickly, in fact, that he walked straight into someone on the street outside, shoving the person in the arm and sending his own bag and the other person's keychain to the ground.

"I'm sorry," he said automatically, looking

at the other for the first time.

It was a girl with long hair. She looked seventeen or eighteen, had very fair skin, and wore thick eyeliner, which made her seem more like an adult.

"What's the big rush?" she said in a tone that was unusually intimidating for a girl.

"I'm sorry, I was in a bit of hurry," apologized Ichiro, bowing all the while. He picked up the keychain, checked that it wasn't dirty, and handed it back to her, noticing her purple manicured nails. Then he picked up his bag and began walking in the direction of Kawaramachi Street.

"Hey, wait a second," the strangely calm voice came from behind him. Surprised, he stopped in his tracks, and turned his head around. It was the girl, gesturing for him to come over with the keychain in her fingers. For a second, he considered running away. But secure in the knowledge that she was only a girl, he called out, "What is it?"

It would have been a lie to say he didn't hope this was his special encounter with a Kyoto woman. But it was a hope that was instantly crushed.

"Don't you 'what is it' me!"

Ichiro feared she was a member of a motor-cycle gang or something like that. "I apologize," he said.

"You think you can get away with anything if you apologize?"

He wondered what she was so upset about, but accepting that he was in the wrong, he apologized again: "Honestly, I'm sorry."

The girl laughed out loud. "Why don't you at least tell me your name."

Ichiro was lost for a response. The thing he hated most about his life was precisely his name.

Every time he gave his parody of a common name, people frowned as if they thought he was kidding. Then they'd realize he wasn't and would hasten to say, "A nice name." The number of times he'd cursed his father for giving him a name that made him a laughing stock—and to make matters worse, his father loved to boast of how he'd chosen "such a fancy name."

"My name is Aoki," said Ichiro, opting to give his surname instead.

"Aoki what?"

He wondered if she somehow knew about his weakness. And when he remained silent, she urged him on like a cat bullying a mouse. "Come on. Aoki what?"

"Aoki, Ichiro," he mumbled. A bead of sweat trickled down his back, but all she did was humph and raise an eyebrow.

"Goodbye then."

Ichiro was taken aback by her reaction, or the lack of it, to be more accurate. But making escape his first priority, he made to walk away.

"Hey, wait a second there, Ichiro."

So she had heard my name, he thought. But her voice was soft now and he froze to the spot.

"Ichiro, where are you going in such a hurry?"

He could tell he was being teased, but something in his heart was being pulled towards her.

"I'm planning to go see the bell at Chion-in temple."

"The bell? What do you mean?" She looked puzzled.

"It's one of the three most famous bells in Japan and it weighs almost 75 tons."

"The three most famous bells? You know some strange things," she said, looking surprised.

"You're not from Kyoto, are you? Kids from around here wouldn't know something like that."

Ichiro felt like they were starting to hit it off, and he began to think this may indeed be one of those special encounters you were supposed to have during your travels. It wasn't bad.

"I'm a high school student from Tokyo. From K High School. I just came to Kyoto to do some historical research, and I thought I'd begin by going to Chion-in, the headquarters of the Pure Land school of Buddhism. I was just leaving the inn and..."

"You're in high school?" Her voice had turned menacing again and Ichiro felt a little intimidated. Nevertheless, he managed to respond:

"I most certainly *am* in high school. May I venture a guess and say that you're a senior?"

"Stop speaking so politely. It's creepy. Anyway, I'm a sophomore so don't insult me."

Ichiro thought she looked a little too old to be a sophomore. But he was more preoccupied by thoughts of how much fun it might be to go around some temples with a streetwise girl like her. Seems to be the kind who gets around, he thought, maybe something exciting might happen. But the words that escaped his mouth were, "I'm sorry, but I think I'll be on my way now."

As if reading his mind, the girl brought her face up close to him and said, "You were thinking dirty thoughts, weren't you."

"N-no, of course not," he spluttered, amazed at how oddly perceptive she was. Then, at that precise moment, a stranger cut in from the side.

"Hey, Jun, what you up to, standing around here? You haven't been showing up at the rallies recently. Slacking off, are you?"

He was wearing a navy blue combat jacket that had "Japanese Spirit" embroidered with silver thread in kanji characters on the back. He also had the character for "Life" embroidered on his rolled-up sleeves. He was clearly a real member of a motorcycle gang. And what was worse, he had three others with him in similar outfits.

"Leave me alone," Jun said.

"Okay. Bye then," Ichiro said at exactly the same moment. It was the first time he'd ever seen a real biker, and he found himself going weak at the knees in this threatening atmosphere.

"Who's this? What's he doing here?"

Ichiro ducked his head instinctively.

"Says he's going to see the bell at Chion-in," Jun answered casually.

"What d'ya mean bell? Are you stupid?"

The guy looked Ichiro up and down. Thinking he'd really gotten himself into a jam now, he began to mumble something like a Buddhist mantra to himself. Although it wasn't a real mantra, but a string of historical facts: "Chion-in was the Shogun's family temple. The current structure dates back to the seventeenth century..."

The guy suddenly put a friendly arm around Ichiro's shoulders and said, "What you mumbling about, you idiot? Hey, instead of going to see some useless bell, why don't we go have ourselves a *real* good *chime*!"

Ichiro couldn't but notice how the guy's head smelled terrible. Breaking into a cold sweat, he mustered up the courage to answer, "I'm fine actually."

"Ah, you're fine with it? Then let's go! Let's

stop wasting time and get down to Kiyamachi."

"I meant I'm fine in the other sense."

"What you rattling on about, huh? Jun, you come too. There's something I need to talk to you about."

Ichiro couldn't possibly escape given the strong grip the guy had on his shoulder. I've only just arrived in Kyoto, he thought, and I'm already in a jam. What should I do? What did I do to deserve this? As his thoughts raced in one direction, his body went where the guy was leading him. He looked to Jun, pleading with his eyes for her help, but she had her nose in the air and ignored him.

"Thanks for today, Ichiro!"

"Yeah, thanks for treating us!"

"See ya, Ichiro!"

"Yeah, you little shit!"

BOY

"Forget your stupid bells and go home to Tokyo!"

Ichiro watched them heading off in high spirits. He stood stunned and all alone in the middle of Kiyamachi Street as drunks passed him by one after another. He'd basically been abducted by the bikers and forced to go bar-hopping to three different places. At each one, he'd waited for the right moment and said, "Um, I think I'll be going now," just to be told, "Come on, we're only getting started, this is practice! The night in Kyoto is just beginning!" What was worse, of course, was the fact that they'd made him pick up the tab at all three places. He'd been milked to the tune of 50,000 yen, and all he'd had were two skewers of grilled chicken and three small glasses of juice. Now his wallet contained just four 1,000 yen bills and a few 100 yen coins.

"What now? I can't even stay at that inn."

He was in a desperate state, with no money to continue his solo travels or to carry out research in Kyoto. Worse still, he couldn't even buy a ticket back to Tokyo with only 4,000 yen on him. Without any particular destination in mind, he walked from Kiyamachi Street to Shijo Street, then staggered over towards the Shinkyogoku area, walking into the first late-night café he saw and ordering a coke.

This is what traveling is all about, it's an adventure, he tried to convince himself, but with no success. I'm hopeless, just like my father says. The thought brought a tear to his eyes. Only the night before, Ichiro's father had scolded him for his poor grades on his midterms. Ichiro had been reading a book on ancient history in his room when suddenly his father called him over.

"You're a real hopeless case," were the first words out of his father's mouth. "I hear that all you ever talk about is history. And that you aren't studying for school at all. If you keep this up, you're going to waste all the opportunities that fine school of yours offers. And you won't be able to get into a decent college, either."

It was unusual for his father to come home without having gone out drinking with his friends, and Ichiro couldn't forget the serious look on his face.

"Life isn't just about entrance exams. There are plenty of other important things to do. And I want to study history."

"I had a friend like you when I was in junior high. He's teaching at a university out in the countryside now. He's always been poor. What's there to gain from doing something like that? You know academia doesn't pay."

It was clear that his father, a successful and hard-working departmental director of a trading house, said this to mean, "Look at the power I have."

"Life isn't all about money or power."

"I'll have none of your lip. You're still a kid, and you'll do what your parents tell you. You might think you've grown up, but you're still a kid. You're just in your third year of junior high, and you have no idea how tough life is. So don't you start telling me about how life is or isn't."

"It's my life, not yours!"

"Say that again. Come on. I said, say it again!" his father yelled.

About to hit him, he was stopped only by Ichiro's mother, who said, "Go back to your room, Ichiro."

Eyes red with tears of frustration, he shouted, "I'm going to live my life my way. No matter what!" and shut himself up in his room. That was when he decided to use his post-exam vacation to visit Kyoto.

Brushing off his mother, he'd left Tokyo just this morning like he was running away from home. The argument with his father was still vivid in his mind and the tears welled up in his eyes again.

He needed desperately to find some work so he could make the money to return to Tokyo. And meanwhile where would he stay? If he called his mother, she'd probably come and pick him up straight away. But there was no way he could do that. He watched his tears drop on the table.

"Hey, you're crying?"

He felt someone tap him on the shoulder. Turning around abruptly, he was surprised to see Jun standing beside him. Immediately, he tried to run away. After all, it was her fault he could no longer stay at the Minamoto Inn or carry out his research in Kyoto. She was nothing but bad luck.

"Wait a second, Ichiro, will you?"

Hearing this, he sat back down again. "I don't have any more money," he said, sounding like he'd lost all belief in the world.

"You're crying because you don't have any more money?"

"Yes."

"Do you have anywhere to stay?"

"No," he said faintly.

"I'm sorry about what happened," consoled Jun.

Now Ichiro was confused. He wondered if this was just another ploy to squeeze yet more money out of him, but he also realized it was the first time he'd ever sat face to face with a girl in a café, even if she was something of a delinquent like Jun. And she was sounding awfully kind.

"I'm sorry."

"It's okay. I've already forgotten about it."

"Then why are you crying?"

For a minute, he didn't know what to say. Then he relaxed a little and began to tell Jun about the fight with his father. As he did, he began to feel a little more cheerful.

"Your parents are real nice, aren't they?" Jun said, obviously impressed.

"Nice? Jun-san, I think you might have misunderstood."

"Don't call me that. Jun is fine. And misunderstanding or not, there's no doubt they're good parents."

"That's not true," responded Ichiro, annoyed.

"You're stubborn, aren't you?" said Jun, before letting out a loud laugh.

"That's not true. I just have a dream," he insisted.

"A dream, huh. So where are you going to

stay tonight?"

Unable to answer the question, he remained silent. Then Jun poked his head with her forefinger. "Why don't you stay at my place?"

"I don't know..."

"Come on, come stay at my place."

"Well, if you're sure. Thank you very much. I'll do that." He made a quick bow with his head and touched the part of it Jun had poked.

"It's nothing fancy, though," she added, then headed straight for the exit.

"Um, Jun, what about the bill?"

"You pay for it, Ichiro."

"Come on, hurry up. It's time to go." And with that Jun gave him a gentle kick to the thigh to rouse him from his slumber.

"Good morning," he yawned. "Can you tell me what the time is?"

"Come on. Wake up. This is your tooth-brush," she said, and dropped on his face a tooth-brush with the name of a hotel clearly printed across it.

The previous night, after leaving the late-night café, Ichiro had followed Jun and stayed at her home on Rokujo-Higashino-Toin Street near Higashi Honganji temple. The street had been empty; small inns and confectionery shops dotted it between regular homes.

When they got close to where she lived, Ichiro couldn't help but ask, "Higashi Honganji is nearby, isn't it," to which Jun responded, "Shut up," showing that her mood had suddenly turned sour. "Here we are."

It was an old townhouse with a sign of a tabi sock outside. Actual split-toe socks lined the inside of the dark store as if they had been acci-dentally left there and long forgotten. And when she led him to a room upstairs, he felt like he was back at the Minamoto Inn.

"It's not much but." Jun sounded a little embarrassed.

Ichiro thought it best to say something. "It's got a real traditional feel to it."

"No need to be polite," Jun retorted with a laugh.

They drank canned beer that Jun brought from the kitchen. Ichiro even had his first cigarette. It wasn't long before he began to feel dizzy and announced that he was going to sleep. Then, forgetting all about the fight with his father and how he'd been swindled out of his money, he fell into a deep and restful sleep.

"Hurry up and get ready. You want to go see temples, right? We'll grab breakfast outside."

"*We'll* grab breakfast outside? Does that mean you're coming too, Jun-san?" Ichiro was now wide awake and joy oozed from his words.

"I promised yesterday, didn't I? That I'd take you around on my bike to make up for having you treat us. And stop calling me Jun-san, will you?"

"Wow. That's a fantastic idea."

"A fantastic idea? You're still a junior high student. Start speaking like one. And hurry up."

As Ichiro folded up the futon as fast as he could, the paper doors suddenly slid open.

"Yoko, you better go to school today. Your teacher came yesterday and said you won't be able to graduate if you keep this up."

It must have been Jun's mother, but she looked much older and more tired than Ichiro's.

"It's none of your business," said Jun. "Ichiro, come on, let's go." The harshness of her tone surprised him.

Finishing off getting ready, Ichiro greeted

the lady. "Good morning. Thank you for your hospitality." But she completely ignored him.

"Ichiro, stop your idle talk, and let's go," Jun prodded and left the room. He rushed down the stairs behind her and the voice of Jun's mother rang out behind them: "Yoko, go to school, okay? Yoko!"

A brand new 250cc bike was parked in front of the shop, looking out of place next to the dingy sign. Ichiro was intrigued by this place and peered into the workshop area, but even in the morning sun, it looked just as dingy as the sign.

The engine started with a roar behind him and Ichiro spun around.

"Hop on."

Already wearing a helmet herself, Jun tossed one over to Ichiro. It was his first time to ride a bike, and feeling somewhat reserved, he placed his hands only lightly on her hips and moved his chest back so he wasn't resting on her back. It was at that moment Jun let out the clutch, unleashing a force that sent Ichiro reeling back and nearly knocked him off the bike.

"Ha ha ha."

He could hear Jun's laughter mixed in with the sound of the engine. Dropping his shyness, he pulled himself in tight to her back and put both arms around her waist. Until then, he had thought of her as a skinny girl. But now he could feel the weight of her breasts above his arms and he found she was bigger than he'd realized.

I can't believe I'm holding a girl in my arms, Ichiro thought. This is what a woman's body feels like! A peculiar satisfaction welled up in him. For the first time since embarking on the journey, he felt glad he'd come.

"Jun, don't you have to go to school?" ventured Ichiro, as they ate breakfast at KFC.

"That's none of your business, is it."

"I guess not. So Jun, your real name is Yoko?"

"Leave me alone. Stop talking and eat."

"But I'm not sure if I should call you Jun or Yoko."

"Jun, of course, you idiot. How can I like a name that my parents just stuck me with?"

"I see what you're saying, but..."

Ichiro thought about his own name. He didn't like his name either, but the reason he didn't like his and she didn't like hers was different. He was still using his real name, too, whereas Jun was faithful to a name of her own. He wanted to tell her this, but decided not to, as it would be too embarrassing.

"What are you thinking? You should decide on what you want to go see first, Ichiro."

"I've already decided. Senbon Shakado."

"Shakado? What's that? Where is it?"

"It's near Kitano-Tenmangu Shrine. Go along Senbon Street, please."

"Why do you know so much about somebody else's town? You must be crazy."

Ichiro felt pleased with himself. He got carried away and began his commentary. "The reason I want to see the Senbon Shakado first is that it's the oldest temple structure in Kyoto city. It was built in the first year of the Antei Era, which was 1227, and it survived the Onin War."

"What are you rattling on about? Let's just go."

Jun had interrupted his explanation, but Ichiro thought he could just continue with the rest once they arrived.

"This is the first time I've ever been here,"

Jun said.

There was nobody else on the quiet premises. They got off the bike and Jun looked around curiously. Then she cried, "Ichiro, Ichiro, what's that, that huge figure?"

"That's Okamesan."

"Looks interesting."

Jun trotted over to look at Okamesan.

"That's not what we came to see," he muttered, but he went and stood in front of the pear-faced statue anyway. There was a notice board explaining the origin of Okame-zuka: "Okame" was the wife of the master builder Takatsugu, who constructed the main temple of Senbon Shakado. During the construction of the temple, her husband had cut one of the pillars too short. She saved him from his mistake by advising him to cut the other pillars down to the same length; however, ashamed that she had interfered with her husband's work, she later committed suicide.

Now that Ichiro thought about it, the main temple did feel like it was slightly lower than the others. Jun noticed too, nodding as she looked at the pillars of the main temple. Mrs. Okame and Jun were kind of similar, Ichiro thought. Not their faces, of course. If he said that, she would no doubt hit him. He just got the feeling that if Okame-san had lived in today's world, she might have been kind of like Jun.

Ichiro left Jun and stood straight in front of the main temple before taking a deep bow. He stared ahead at the 760 years of history he had come all this way to see and felt his heart being cleansed and purified by it.

"Boo!" said Jun, bumping him in the back. "What are you thinking about, with such a serious look on your face?"

"I was having an encounter with history."

"Don't be an idiot," said Jun, but she seemed to be waiting for him to continue.

"I just feel good when I stand in front of something so old and big like this. This has been standing in the same place and breathing the same air for eight centuries. I'm deeply moved by that. Of course I'm also impressed by the great power of leaders and religion, but coming face to face with history like this really moves me. I really want to become a historian…"

As he spoke, Ichiro was moved by his own words, and his voice cracked. But Jun didn't laugh.

"I see. But because we have so many of these old things all over the place, our roads are narrow and everywhere it stinks of incense. What's so great about shrines and temples? I hate

BOY

Kyoto. What you see on the surface and what lies underneath are completely different. People are always saying things behind your backs, and sabotaging your plans. I hate it. The only people who get to play around are the guys from the temples. The monks are the ones with the money. They act all self-important, but really they're all perverted. You wouldn't believe the number of times..." Jun choked on her words and stopped herself. "I'm sorry Ichiro. I understand how you feel, and there's nothing wrong with that at all. But I'm me. And no matter how much I try, I can't like this city. My home. My parents. My siblings. Anyway, enough of that, let's go. Where do you want to go next?"

Ichiro had been overwhelmed by the seriousness of Jun's tone. He felt like she knew a separate world of adults that he knew nothing about. It was true, he was still a kid...

"Ichiro, what do you want to see next? We can go anywhere in this small city in no time by bike."

"Ryoanji," he answered quietly.

Jun laughed. "Even I know that one. The place with all the rocks." It was genuinely happy laughter that made Ichiro laugh as well, and their giggles resonated through the dark of the main temple, traveling past arrow marks that had been there since the Onin War, before fading into the distance.

At Ryoanji, they had a small incident. In a garden of white sand designed to look like the sea, fifteen rocks were laid out in groups of seven, five and three. Ichiro explained that if you sat down and counted the number of rocks, it looked like there were only fourteen.

"That can't be true. Fifteen is fifteen," said

Jun, and she began counting from all different angles. She looked so intent as she did so that Ichiro began counting the rocks as well using a mechanical pencil. But as he was doing this, the pencil slipped from his hand and fell onto the sand. He stretched his arm out to try and pick it up, but he couldn't reach it. So he stretched out his leg to try to drag it closer. Just as he was about to reach it, Jun called out to him from the other side of the hallway. "Ichiro, what are you doing?"

Surprised, he lost his balance and his foot touched the sand below. Quick as a flash he pulled it up, but too late—a clearly visible mark had been left in the sand. Right at that moment, a monk on cleaning duty happened to pass by and noticed the mark immediately.

"Who did this to our Cultural Property?" he said, glaring at Ichiro. "What's your problem?"

Ichiro didn't know what to do.

"Come on, Ichiro, let's get out of here!"

Jun pulled Ichiro by the hand away from the spot where he'd frozen still, and started running for the exit.

"Hey, wait!" The monk was calling after them, but Ichiro didn't care. Once they were outside the gates, the two of them looked at each other and burst out laughing.

Although it was supposed to be the season for school excursions, there were not many people in Sagano on that end-of-October weekday, and it had the perfect paths for riding tandem through bamboo forests.

This is where the woman in yesterday's video was walking, Ichiro noted. Of course, it was just a film, but the woman in front of him now was real. I'm so glad I came to Kyoto, he mused, tightening his grip around Jun's waist and burying his face in her back. He could smell her sweet and sour scent, and he felt a stirring in his crotch. Just then, Jun suddenly pulled on the brakes, making him hold on to her all the more.

"You dumb pervert. What are you doing?"

Jun hit Ichiro on his helmet, but fortunately she was laughing. She parked the bike and they had lunch at a nearby soba shop.

While they were eating, Jun asked him, "Ichiro, you got a girlfriend?"

Ichiro choked on his soba and almost coughed it out. He said, "Yes, well, before, but I'm on my own now." He found himself trying to act cool despite himself. I can't be honest like Jun, he thought.

Jun just said, "Is that right."

Ichiro thought of asking her, "How about you, Jun," but the answer seemed so obvious he couldn't ask.

"Let's not go to any more temples. Let's go

for a ride instead," Jun said cheerfully, as if to change the mood.

"Sounds like a good idea. May I suggest Kurama?"

"Ichiro, enough of that. You've really got to stop talking so politely to me."

"Certainly, yes."

"You're never going to learn, are you?"

Starting from Kyomi Pass, the two of them rode through the northern mountains of Kyoto to Kurama and on to Mt. Hiei. Then they passed Takaragaike Pond which, according to Jun, was haunted by ghosts (although Ichiro insisted he'd never read about anything real of the sort). As they passed the Kyoto International Conference Hall and were about to go into the tunnel, they suddenly heard a loud noise behind them.

Honk, Honk, Ho-nk! It was the sound of several unusual horns.

BOY

Ichiro turned his head and was horrified to see a motorcycle gang chasing after them at quite a speed. Jun must have noticed too, as she immediately sped up, zooming through the tunnel, trying to escape into Kitayama Street. But the group of several bikers caught up to them in no time and were sticking right with them. Ichiro recognized the guy leading the pack—the one who'd spoken to Jun yesterday and who'd ripped Ichiro off for 50,000 yen. Jun sped on, ignoring a red light, but on Kitayama-Obashi Bridge over Kamogawa river, their path was blocked. They were dragged off the bike.

"You're the kid from yesterday, aren't you! So, you think you can mess around with my woman, huh? Come on then. Let's finish this right here!"

The biker grabbed the collar of Ichiro's varsity jacket and drove a knee sharply into his stomach. And although Ichiro had wanted to fight like a man in front of Jun, the blow from the knee had put him down on the ground before he could do a thing.

"Stop it Minoru," screamed Jun. "Stop it you guys! I'm the one who invited him out! Leave him alone!"

"You damn fool!" Minoru hit Jun hard in the face. "You think you can ride around on my bike and get away with this kind of crap? Dragging this kid along? You ever do this again and I'll really make you pay! Understand?" Then he hit her again while the others rained a volley of kicks on Ichiro as he lay on the ground.

"I'm sorry, Ichiro. We were having so much fun. It all got messed up."

The two of them washed the mud and blood from their faces in the Kamogawa river and sat down on the bank facing the sun setting in the western hills.

"Don't worry, I had a really fun time," Ichiro said, fighting back the pain in his abdomen. "Jun, don't just sit there. Say something."

But she didn't say anything. Instead, she leaned her head against Ichiro's shoulder, and they sat together like that for a while in silence. Jun was the first to speak.

"Ichiro, I have to tell you something," she said. "I was lying. I'm not a sophomore. I'm in my third year of junior high, too."

Ichiro couldn't understand why she'd chosen to lie, but managed to reply: "Is that right? I thought you might be."

"I've been a bad apple since my first year in junior high, and I got screwed by Minoru in the summer of my second year. So now I belong to

Minoru."

Ichiro failed to find words this time. All he could do was nod in response, as blood gushed out from where "got screwed" stuck into his heart.

"It can't be helped. People are born with a certain level of luck. I'm one of the luckier ones. You've no idea how many of my friends have died." Then she started to cry. All Ichiro could do was nod his head.

"If I can stay alive until next year, and I'm able to graduate from junior high, I'm thinking of leaving Kyoto. I don't want to live in this narrow place anymore."

"Where will you go?" Ichiro's voice was dry and hoarse.

"Tokyo. I can't keep living like this. I want to go to technical school and find a good job."

Jun brought her head up from Ichiro's

shoulder, then picked up a pebble and threw it toward the river. Watching the flight of the pebble, she murmured, "I'm leaving and going to Tokyo"—like she'd definitely made up her mind.

"That's a good idea. When you come to Tokyo, you can stay at my place."

"How could I possibly stay at a home like yours that's all proper? You just keep on getting dumber."

Ichiro didn't say yes or no. He just felt terribly desolate. It was the first time in his life that he'd ever felt so desolate.

"Ichiro, you go home to Tokyo tomorrow," said Jun. Without waiting for him to answer, she began walking downriver along the bank.

Ichiro could hear Jun's breathing as she slept on the other side of the paper doors. It was as regular as clockwork. He could hear this girl the same age as him sleeping soundly. A girl with a life entirely different from his.

"She's amazing," Ichiro sighed, and truly thought so. The history of Senbon Shakado was amazing, but Jun was just as amazing, he was sure of it. But those words "got screwed" still remained stuck in his chest. Jun had been screwed. She hadn't done the screwing, she had gotten screwed. He was certain that Jun had said it that way. That she had gotten screwed. Thinking so somehow eased the pain a little. And without knowing quite why, he pushed his right hand down inside his pants.

The next morning it was raining. When Ichiro awoke to the sound of raindrops hitting the roof, Jun had already left her room.

What now? How am I going to get home? Ichiro's usual worried look returned to his face. But right at that moment, a cheerful Jun walked in, the rain dripping from her long hair.

"Ichiro, we're going, hurry up and get ready."

Ichiro did as he was told, getting ready and stepping out into the rain.

"We're using the shop's bicycle today," said Jun, pointing to a black bicycle with the words "Tagawa Tabi Shop" painted on it in white.

"Hurry up and hop on," she said, sounding high-spirited but looking rather forlorn.

"All right, but where are we going?"

"Just shut up and hang on. After I send you back on your way to Tokyo, I'm going to school today."

"You'll be late for school if you do that. You don't have to worry about me."

"Better late than never, right?" quipped Jun, giving a small laugh. Ichiro just nodded.

Striding onto the back seat of the bike,

Ichiro opened the umbrella Jun had pushed on him, and held it up just as she told him to, so that they were sharing it like a couple, even though they were sitting on the front and back of a bicycle. Ichiro was about to put his free arm around Jun's waist like the day before but hesitated. I guess, he thought, it's not necessary on a bicycle. But now he felt something was lacking. The bicycle began moving forward, making its way slowly through the streets of Kyoto. Realizing that his journey was coming to an end, Ichiro felt sentimental. He looked at Jun's hips and wished time would stop. He gazed at the shape of her behind as it moved a little to the right, a little to the left, then a little to the right in time with the pedals. Just when he was saying to himself, "Oh, how I wish I could touch that," Jun suddenly hit the brakes and told Ichiro to get off.

"O-okay." Ichiro hopped off immediately, imagining she'd guessed at his dirty thoughts.

"Run alongside me, will you?"

He was right, she *had* seen through his thoughts. It was like she had eyes on the back of her head. Dejected, he ran alongside the bike for about a hundred meters or so, when Jun stopped the bicycle again. Ichiro wondered what could be the problem this time.

"You can get back on now," she said. Seeing the puzzled look on Ichiro's face, she laughed and said, "Police box," nodding her chin in the direction they'd come from. So that was what—Ichiro jumped happily back onto the bicycle.

Jun took him to the entrance of the Meishin Expressway, where she hoped she could stop a truck and have Ichiro hitchhike his way back to Tokyo. She parked the bicycle on the sidewalk, pushed the umbrella onto him, told him to wait there, and loped off towards the road. Ichiro watched her stick out her fist with her thumb up as trucks drove by one after the other, splashing her as they passed, making her dripping wet.

"Jun, you've done enough," called Ichiro. "I'll do the rest myself. You're going to be really late for school." He couldn't watch her continue and ran over to her with the umbrella, but Jun wouldn't listen.

"Don't you know anything, Ichiro? Trucks are more likely to stop for a girl on her own. Just leave this to me."

Crestfallen, he headed back to where he'd been standing and waited for another ten minutes. But in all that time, still no cars had stopped, and Jun was now soaked to her underwear.

BOY

I can't let her, Ichiro thought. He ran over to her. "I'm serious. You've done enough. You'll catch a cold, Jun. I'll do it."

Jun turned around and yelled at him. "I told you to shut up and watch from over there." She pushed him over to the side of the road, and raising both arms in the air, jumped out onto the middle of the road.

"Watch out!" cried Ichiro.

Trucks were zooming past uncomfortably close and drivers shouted, "Get off the road, idiot!" as they passed by. Ichiro found himself praying to something and found that he had unconsciously clasped his hands together.

After another thirty or so vehicles had whizzed past, a large truck with a Kanagawa number plate finally stopped. Ichiro watched Jun pleading with the driver with her hands placed together over her head. When it looked as if they'd concluded their negotiations, Jun came running over.

"What a guy. Making me beg like that. But it's all set, Ichiro. He said you'll make it to Tokyo by early evening."

"Jun, thank you, I..." Ichiro's eyes were filled with tears.

"Don't be silly. We'll just have to see each other again."

And with those words, Jun put her hands on Ichiro's shoulders and kissed him lightly on the mouth—the rain-drenched lips felt so hot.

"I'm not going to wait forever!" bellowed the truck driver. "If you're getting in, you'd better get over here now!"

"See you again, Jun."

Jun handed him a small paper package. "Something for the road. Eat it in the truck."

She walked on over to the sidewalk. Ichiro

got into the passenger's seat, closed the door, rolled down the window, and shouted, "Thank you Jun!"

She looked small and thin as she waved up at Ichiro. She's just a third-year junior high school student, he remembered. Just like me. The truck began to move. Ichiro stuck his head out of the window and into the rain and watched Jun grow smaller and smaller.

"Don't you think it's about time you closed the window?" The forty-something driver kept his eyes on the road as he asked in a baritone, "Is that your girlfriend? She's cute."

"No, she isn't, but…"

Ichiro felt a lump in the back of his throat and felt tears on his face again as he rolled up the window. Leaning over to see the wing mirror, he found in it the back of a tiny, tiny Jun walking away. He unfolded the paper package she had given to him and a sweet cinnamon scent filled the cabin.

"Is that *yatsuhashi*?" said the driver. Ichiro opened the small box and found about twenty cinnamon sweets lined up neatly inside.

"Why don't we try them then?" said the driver, casually reaching over with his hand, picking up three pieces, and throwing them in his mouth.

Ichiro watched his thick fingers, tough and leathery as you'd expect a truck driver's to be.

And he thought, People like him, they're the adults.

About the Author

Takeshi Kitano is the recipient of the Golden and Silver Lion Prizes, Venice Film Festival, for *Hana-bi* and *Zato-ichi*. He is also the author of many prose works ranging from memoirs and fiction to social criticism and interview collections. Before he achieved worldwide fame he was one of Japan's most popular television personalities, which he continues to be, thanks to his sharp eye and irreverent sense of humor. *Boy* is the first literary work by Japan's "Renaissance man" to be translated into English. Mr. Kitano lives and works in Tokyo.

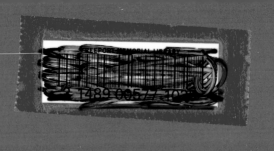